Realm Walker

Soul of Malice

Elle Klass

Soul of Malice

Copyright©2025 by Elle Klass
Published by Books by Elle, Inc.
ISBN: 978-1-951017-50-7
All rights reserved
Editor Dawn Lewis

Author's Disclaimer

REALM WALKER

Books in the Realm Walker Series
In the Shadows
The Land of Lost Souls
Hidden Passages
The Ring of Betrayal

Realm Walker Prequel
Heart of Darkness
Soul of Malice

Other Realm Walker Companion Books
The Origin: Marya's Journal
Soul Fire
Life After Death

Realm Walker World Books – coming soon!
Love at Frost Bite
Accidental Ghost: Soul Catcher Vol.1

Other Young Adults Series
The Bloodseekers
Zombie Girl
Hidden Journals
Baby Girl

The Inbetween
Sier.
Thraves
Canida
Provence City
Drakonia
Aradia
Verboten
Navarin

1

Realm Leaders Holocall

Cyrus's emotions are out of control. She feels only a portion of the pain he does, and it is overwhelming. The drop of her blood running through his veins has diminished in strength. Each wave of sorrow that overcomes him stops her cold in her tracks and thoughts. When Ryel died, his agony hit her like a shockwave and rumbled through the realms.

M'ra's soul mourns with him as his grief is enormous. She understands his attraction. Despite the young woman's apparent beauty, she was something different, something worth preserving and fighting for. She was the only hybrid M'ra ever knew about in her long life, born and belonging to all seven middle realms. Cyrus called her a natural born realm walker.

His grief rocks every corner of the realms. The purebloods are anxious and fearful. The woman's death seems a waste, but sadness has a way of progressing change. *Will it be enough? How far will Cyrus go?* Those questions tarry on M'ra's mind as she joins the other realm leaders in the holocall. They were willing to meet, not with him, but with each other. It's the first step.

The Navarin queen, golden sun on her blonde hair, glows with the backdrop of the bright sky. Her blue eyes narrow on the Canidan leader. "He's dangerous and you can't keep your lycans in line. The damage he can do would be irreparable." Her words reflect the tremor that rippled through each realm when Cyrus fought three other realm walkers, showing his individual strength had developed beyond theirs combined, his misery a conduit to his strength.

"Lycans are free to come and go. I think the lycan's death is suitable punishment," the large lycan fumes, chest puffing up like a bird. It was Ryel who killed the lycan, attacking him in her wolf form in Provence, before the arrow to her chest took her down. It was the last of her incredible strength. It was after the lycan attempted to shoot her or Cyrus with a deadly arrow. She exposed all the realm walkers and hybrids when she did that. Purebloods can't perform level 3 magic in Provence, nor can most hybrids, but she was special.

The meeting with the realm leaders doesn't appear to be going anywhere. They all agreed to meet to discuss how to move forward, maybe come to a consensus with the young realm walkers and hybrids, and the realm leaders are taking bites out of each other. They are a stubborn lot.

Even through the holocall their loathing for one another is apparent. "We aren't here to bark at each other. You should feel ashamed in striking at each other in times of death. We do need to be concerned with Cyrus and practice vigilance, but we need to acknowledge his plight. What is it they want? Can we meet them halfway? We should call a meeting with him." M'ra suggests.

"I will do no such thing!" barked the Chief of Thraves. "He is my realm walker and will report to me or lose his life in Thraves." *What life?* The one he is fighting to change, willing to risk his life and others to change. M'ra's frustration with the stubborn realm leaders mounts and she isn't sure how long she can keep it together. Showing aggravation won't do any good. She grips her hands together so tight her nails dig into her palms and draw blood. It helps her focus her attention and push down her rising frustration. The sting of pain centers her thoughts, a quality she and Cyrus share. Something she hadn't known until a drop of her blood was inserted into his transfusion when he returned from Lols injured.

Vampire blood has many qualities, unknown to others outside of Drakonia. Its healing properties are phenomenal but can't raise the dead. Cyrus, holding a dead Ryel on the lobby floor of the tower in Drakonia, tears pouring from his eyes, is an image she'll never get out of her head, nor the burn of his pain. The protest he led was peaceful. He didn't want to take what others have. He didn't want war. He only wanted equality, and not only for himself but others like him. No one would ever call him humble; cocky, self-assured, clever, powerful…but not humble. His goals, lofty and probably self-serving, could also benefit everyone if only the realm leaders would listen.

It's the leader of Verboten who finally speaks sense, making M'ra feel as though she isn't alone in defending Cyrus and her attempts to get ears to listen to him and the hybrids. "There are no laws governing extrarealm relations. Any laws that existed centuries ago are gone as governments changed and Provence has no laws or regulations. I think we should hear him out. It could be something that would benefit all of us." Her yellow tail feathers rise above the back of her head.

"You treat hybrids with disdain. No one likes or appreciates a hypocrite," the supreme dragon of Sier says with sarcasm to the troll. He is right, yet this meeting is about changing their ways.

Drakonia is the only realm that treats hybrids with respect. In fact, they are treated well yet they still protested. Because it's about more. As a dictator, M'ra can modify the laws in her land without consent yet she doesn't need to. The vampires support her. Hands in her lap, the nail slices already healed on her hands. The plight of realm walkers and their claim to Provence hasn't been unspoken over the years. No realm walker had professed their claim the way Cyrus and the hybrids did but the words were spoken often between realm walkers. Strength is found in numbers which the realm walkers never had, whether by Merla's design or not. Cyrus and the hybrids are smart.

"Aradia has many hybrids. It's best for them to hide in the thick forests. We turn our heads to them, pretend they don't exist. I'm open to negotiations. Why don't we take a vote of those in favor of meeting with Cyrus?" Elves are very democratic in their government, and generous. Their young realm walker is the only one of the young generation not to get involved in the protest, not because of fear but because she's content and a rule follower. Cyrus isn't. He is a natural born leader.

The elven leader raises her dainty hand, "I vote yes. Who's with me?"

M'ra raises her hand as does the leader of Verboten and, to her surprise, the Canidan leader. He's lost the most between Ryel and the lycan who killed her. Animosity in his ranks, among his people.

The dragon, fae queen, and chief of Thraves refuse. It is settled. The four of them will meet with Cyrus and the hybrids and, with any luck, the others will come around.

2

An entire week has passed since my world imploded. In Ryel's death, my rage flared and damage followed. Energy ripped through my core like a seismic wave and flooded every realm, weakening the veils. I don't care if the realms fall or if I'm the cause.

My body and heart are drained. I haven't risen from my chair or left my inbetween world. I ignore them, all of them, let them sort their own problems or not. I lack any desire to care. We made so much progress, yet it seems meaningless without Ryel at my side. Her violet soul sphere glows bright and hot from the home I made for it on the shelf.

My rage flares with grief. When I close my eyes, she is all I see. My essence torments me day in and day out. I no longer care about anything. Nothing. My soul is a numb void, deep and dark.

A gentle voice slides into my head and the jelly comicay on my wrist flashes green. It temporarily disperses my thoughts of Ryel but they don't leave completely. *Four realm leaders are willing to meet with you. Join us in a holocall.* M'ra. *Why does she care?* Is it her own guilt? She warned me someone would die and I ignored her. Confident the protest would be peaceful, and it was. We didn't riot or rise in anger.

That guilt belongs to the lycans. They killed her, meant to kill us both, but she attacked before an arrow could pierce me. Stupid. I was stupid. I knew the lycans were angry, had words with one. Why didn't I shield us? An arrow would have bounced, no harm done and she'd still be alive, not a violet sphere glowing on a shelf in my inbetween room.

Guilt, M'ra feels it, or is it my grief? My pain like I've been run over by a vehicle in Lols. Its tires pressing me, squashing me, flattening on repeat. What are hybrids and realm walkers to her that she's leading the diplomacies in my stead with the realm leaders? Her own guilt. She betrayed me, the cause, and wants to fix it.

She can't, no one can. Ryel is gone. The light inside, the glint of sun on her blonde locks, her vexing smile gone. My rage is tempered. I feel only sadness and emptiness. I wanted to destroy everything. Now I want to lie in this chair and waste away into oblivion, not plead our case.

When I don't respond she speaks again. *I understand a portion of your pain. It is small but real. My blood is still pumping through your veins. Ryel was special. Don't make her death worthless. Find the strength in you to fight.*

I let out a strangled breath and lift my eyes to Ryel's soul sphere. M'ra is right. Ryel was a fighter and wouldn't be proud of me right now. She'd force me out of this chair. Hate boils through me. It's M'ras fault, my fault for not listening or asking the right questions. Regardless, she is right. Damn her! I can't let Ryel's death be forgotten and unworthy. She believed in me and our fight from the beginning. She came to me. *When?* I respond.

In four days. Gather your people, your strength, and your ideas. Strength. I'm in short supply of that.

Reuniting with the realm walkers isn't on my list of to dos. I'd rather eat tacks after their betrayal. They ganged up and finally used the power they were born with to stop me from killing the lycans responsible for Ryel's death. I never want to see them again or I may kill them.

My loathing of them has no limits; Marilisa, Jine, Hackey, but not Lamont or Shiane. I will meet with them. I can do that without enacting my revenge, but maybe I need that hate to feel anything. Ryel's beautiful body, laid in a dirt bed in Lols, flashes in my mind. Flower petals dancing on the wind. It was my last moments with her flesh and blood lifeless body before returning to my room and I hold on to the moment, devour its sorrow.

I have no want to enter Provence and be bombarded with memories of Ryel's death and don't think I have the strength to enact revenge on the realm walkers responsible for keeping me from revenge on the lycans, so I sequester the realm walkers through a holocall.

"How are you doing?" Lamont asks, sincerity reflected in his tone and features. He is my friend, or at least didn't fight against me.

My face holds no expression. It is dead and lifeless, my voice monotone. "I am doing as well as anyone could expect under the circumstances." I pause. Tiny worry lines dimple in his forehead. "You were true. You had my back. The others, I don't trust them after they attempted to stop me."

His bulky frame shifts uneasily. "It wasn't supposed to turn violent. They didn't want you paying for the crime of death, even Marilisa. I couldn't get on board with them. I wanted the lycans dead too for what they did, but I couldn't stop you. I felt weak in my actions."

"They weren't strong!" I say, condemning their actions, emotion filling my voice. "I don't trust them anymore and I don't fully trust Shiane. She's spent too much of her life surrounded by fae. I want you with me when I meet with the realm leaders."

His thick eyebrows lower. "I don't think I'm the best choice. We should bring in a hybrid from each realm, someone chosen by the hybrids of their realm that will show them we want to work together to create something better."

I nod and Shiane's face blinks to my side as she enters the holocall. I didn't invite her and flick my gaze to Lamont who wears a guilty expression. She offers a warm, heartfelt smile. She hadn't betrayed me. "It's really good to see you. I've been worried. Many of us have."

Of course they have. Not really, not about me, but what damage my anger might cause. Might I rip the realms apart at the seams, destroy everything? I felt the power, it was incredible and now it's flat. The edge to her voice says more, maybe it's the hybrids, because it isn't the realm walkers. They think they lost their leader.

I decide I won't boot her from the call. She did warn us when she discovered the shells given to us by the fae queen were spying devices. "The realm leaders of Verboten, Aradia, Drakonia, and Canida want to meet." At the mention of Canida they squirm. The lycans are responsible and my deepest desire is that they feel guilt beyond any pain I've suffered. It is their kind – lycans – who killed Ryel and with the exact weapons others used on them in wars past. "And I want to thank both of you for not betraying me like the others did."

Her words mimic Lamont's as she makes excuses for the others' behavior, but my hate for the other realm walkers doesn't wane. It is strong, running deep into my heart and soul. The self-righteous traitors led by the most haughty and sanctimonious of them all – Marilisa. I envision gripping her arms and legs with energy and pulling until she's torn apart at the seams. Her entrails dangling from what's left of her torso, blood spilling to the dirt.

My nose twitches and my eyes narrow involuntarily when my comicay blinks three more times and the other realm walkers of my generation join us. I rest my eyes on Marilisa and narrow my gaze, stabbing into them with virtual poison-tipped daggers. Her long hair flashes pink from the fuchsia walls of the room she's sitting. Our relationship never one of friendship and her beauty the only reason I toyed with her and even now, as much as I want to destroy her, envisioning her death without her present was easy, in her presence I can't see myself ripping her limb from limb.

I've known her all my life, and I know all her faces, worked with her since our realm walker training began and her expression isn't one of apology but it is one of anguish. *Is her woe due to Ryel's death or my destruction?* It isn't fear or even asking for my forgiveness. My rage flares and strength I haven't felt in days returns. I want to hate her and I can't, which infuriates me. *Why is she even here?* At no point in the planning of anything was she present.

Jine and Hackey have a hard time resting their eyes on me. My gaze is met with shifts in their eyes. They should be ashamed for what they did, trying to stop me. I take a deep, cleansing breath and state my business without formalities. "Four realm leaders want to meet. I think it would be best to do this democratically and have each of your realms choose a diplomat, not you," I emphasize, "to join me in a holocall." Lamont's advice is sound and worthy of use.

"Which realms?" Shiane asks, her voice squeaky with uncertainty.

"Verboten is one, Aradia," I shift my gaze to Marilisa and stare into her disgusting pure soul, "Drakonia, and Canida."

Hackey blinks awkwardly, as if surprised. He should be. The lycans aren't a people I can stomach right now unless I learn to breathe dragon fire and burn their realm to the ground.

"If we can get them to listen, that's our best way to get the others on board. Right now, its just talks, but that can lead to cooperation," Jine says in her best upbeat voice.

I steady my gaze on the others in the holocall, especially Marilisa. *Why is she here?* Aradia, that's why she's here, to further betray me. As their realm walker, this is her assignment. I'm sure of it. There's no other explanation. Her lack of apology and words say more than if she'd spoken. I was sent to Lols to clear any vampire wrong doings. She is here to get the inside scoop. Good!

We spend the next several minutes discussing ways to entice the hybrids to choose one diplomat until we all agree realm votes is the most democratic. Each hybrid will come with a list of grievances, and I will come prepared with demands for Provence and the law. The blue-prints will come later.

The call ends and my thoughts revert to M'ra. I blamed her call on guilt but there's something more. She is the Minister of the vampires, yet lowered herself to contacting me personally. She didn't use Preston as a courier as she has in the past. *Why?*

It's her blood that saved me in the transfusion. A single drop, also allowing her to connect with me, feel my emotions, think fragments and moments of my thoughts. In Ryel's death she spoke to me, directly to me, as I stood in the lobby of the tower.

She warned me in person, in her office in the high tower, that someone would die. A privilege bestowed only on her most trusted. I entered that office ready to blackmail her in a holocall. Instead, she told me the story of realm walkers with knowledge and passion beyond her young years when the realm walkers were created. How old was she then? She couldn't have been more than a tween, a hybrid child.

I am the forbidden fruit of the lust between two realm walkers. My mother of Thraves and father of Drakonia. It isn't a secret a realm walker's first intercourse leads to a realm walker child who will take their place. It is how the fae curse continues. M'ra knew of her realm walker's sin, Preston, my biological father's sin. When he dies, her realm will forever be realm walker less and the other realms will know the vampires' shame. When I offered her Ryel as a realm walker she denied it. M'ra isn't concerned about the other realm leaders or their gossip.

Is her help in fighting for realm walkers' and hybrids' equality because of her shame or in spite of it? If we are free then it won't matter that her realm has no future realm walker. A different thought hits me, maybe she's trying to obtain what rightfully belongs to Drakonia as much as Thraves — me.

There's only one place to possibly find the answers, aside from time travel, which even I haven't figured out. It is time to visit the unsettled spirits of the dead.

3

There is one way into the Otherworld, then there is my way. It is the one place I've never visited. Deep in the belly of Crest, meters below the lowest point in Thraves, below the lowest point in Drakonia, far beneath CIU. It is the dungeon of death, holding the impure and disquieted souls from the beginning of time.

I don't want Death's permission or knowledge of my visit, nor the harvesters guarding the gate. As a collector of magical items, I have my hands on an ascendant. They all go to one location; the Otherworld, or at

least they are rumored to. There is one said to
take someone to Tranquility, but I only own a
piece of it. There are two halves connected
with a seed from the Serenity Tree. The pieces
spread far and wide before it could be tested.

The one I hold in my hand is a metal
ball. Ryel held it once. I smooth my thumb
over the top as if I can feel her warmth.
Disappointed when I don't. The cold metal of
the ball offers no relief from my pain.
Clutching it in the palm of my hand, I chant,
"Take me past the gates into the realm of the
dead."

The ball heats up and air swarms from
all directions, lifting me off the ground and
enveloping me, similar to portalling. Tucked
inside, I spin quicker and quicker until I'm
unable to see anything as I am moving too
fast. The vortex slows then stops. Air rushes
away from me and shadows swim around my
feet. I don't have Death's permission to be
here, not that it would make me impervious to
the wishes of the dead.

Clutching the metal ball, cold to the
touch now, I stick it in my pocket for the ride
home. The sky above black with a sprinkling
of gray, withered, leafless trees sporadically
dotting the wasteland. The ground, lifeless
loose dirt. Nothing living can grow from it.
The Otherworld is a dangerous place. Anyone
who spends their life in Thraves knows not to
speak but to listen to the dead. They will

answer your thoughts. Incomprehensible whispers murmur through the air as shadows sweep over the dirt and scatter away from my steps.

Focusing my mind, I close my eyes and will words related to vampires. The hisses increase in volume until they clear. As if spoken directly into my ear, I hear the word 'vampire', followed by a hiss that sounds like 'you can bring her back'.

My ears shuffle through the whispers and I hear it again, louder in my ear. 'You can bring her back'. The words drown out everything else.

They are trying to get into my head. I squeeze my eyes shut and listen. The phrase keeps repeating until it's all I can hear, and memories of Ryel flood my head. I fight it and push the energy away, but my strength is greatly diminished in the land of death and from lack of food. I have no power here.

I feel vulnerable, like a commoner from Lols. A weakling with no connection to magic. The voice speaks in my ear again, this time loud enough it echoes through my soul. As a gut reaction I nearly turn my head. My harvester training stops me. 'Don't ever look at them. Don't ever speak to them'. The moment one acknowledges them they have power and will twist your will.

Running, shadows swarming my feet, the voice reverberates through all of the

Otherworld. 'You can bring her back.' From the darkness and through the fog a form appears. I turn my head to avoid looking at it before it catches my gaze. Something touches my skin, her hands rub against my arms and under my chin, around my ear. Her light floral scent fills the air and it feels real, as if she's there. I remind myself; they are messing with your head. Ryel is dead and not in the Otherworld. Her bright violet soul sphere is in your inbetween world, safe from the dead.

Lips touch mine, her lips. Shock radiates through my core, enters my soul, and my eyes involuntarily open. Her form stands before me. Her blonde braids fall over her ears and touch her shoulders. Her soft hand brushes my cheek, electricity and desire tingle. Her shining golden-green eyes push the shadows and fog away, glowing bright. I swallow. No, this isn't her.

"You can bring me back. We can be together again." Her voice rings. I miss the sound of her voice.

I attempt to blink her away but can't. She is here. Her hands touch my waist, wrap around me. *How?*

"I can only exist here for now. But you can change that," she says and kisses my cheek, the other cheek. Her lips sweep against mine.

"How?" *Shit!* I did it, the unthinkable. The first thing all harvesters learn about the

Otherworld and impure souls. Harvesting 101 basics. I interacted with the dead. But nothing happened. She is still here standing in front of me. My hands roam her curves and valleys, desperate for more.

She isn't an illusion. My lips clash against hers; hungry, wanting, desperate. Her tongue moves with mine. She is flesh and blood. Real. She pulls away, our eyes lock, and I bury my hands in the back pockets of her pants and press her against me. I don't care about the curse. I want the one thing we never did. My hands move up her shirt, touch her soft skin.

My lips trail greedily over her neck. I need her. I grab her hand and press it to my groin. When she doesn't respond with her hands in my pants, I lift my face from her neck and meet her gaze. Her lips part and speak words that make no sense. "Go to Drakonia, to the Abandoned Valley, there you will find the scythe of immortality." They sound like her, but don't.

I step away. "No, you're not real."

"You trapped my body here. With the scythe you can return my soul to my body so we can be one again."

Impossible. But is it? Do my eyes and hands deceive me? "How do I know you are you?"

She steps forward, pressing her lips to mine, sliding her fingers down the front of my jeans. Images of Ryel, her beautiful face and smile, her touch lingering on my skin, her laughter and moans of pleasure fill my ears, my mind. They course through my soul and connect. "I'll do it," I mumble through breathless kisses as her fingertips touch me, weaken me.

My breath catches and a burning sensation fills my lungs and spreads through my body until my legs, arms, chest, and privates are on fire. I stumble backwards, clutching my throat, my eyes open. They widen, as her form is no more, its place taken with a shadow. Its red eyes staring at me. It is too late. I've welcomed in a wraith, allowed it to trick me.

If I can portal now, maybe I can stop it. I stretch out my hand and send out my energy. A teal light sparks. I try again and again. The light sparks and dies each time. I can't create a portal, much less move, as they wind me in their web. I reach into my pocket to collect the ball but shadows wrap around my arms, pinning them to my sides. I have no power here.

No! My mind screams as the last of the wraith coils inside me. The shadows let me go, unwinding from my chest and arms and spread across the lifeless dirt of the Otherworld. The wraith is a powerful entity of the dead.

Realm Walker

It can't harm me outside of the Otherworld, as they need a host, but here I am on its turf. It can do as it wants, even manifest itself into a physical form. Wraiths are unharvested dark souls that roam between the world of the dead and the living. I've broken the harvester rule. The one rule we learn from infancy. Don't speak to the dead.

'Don't trust the dead, my instructors always warned. They are fickle and want only for themselves. What is in it for him? The wraith mentioned Drakonia and a scythe. Why does it want me to use it on Ryel? Or was that to manipulate me? Will it come back as Ryel? "No!" My screams of protest echo through the Otherworld.

Take us to Drakonia. A deep voice rises inside me. It's not my voice but female.

"What's in it for you?"

Its laughter shakes my body. *You will know when the time comes.*

That isn't an answer. "I didn't come here for a scythe. I want to know why the minister of Drakonia has any interest in me."

I will tell you once you have the scythe.

Its words meld with my mind as I clutch the ball and whisper, "Take me past the gates to the land of the living."

4

The abandoned desert is the area of Drakonia untouched by vampires. It is said to be haunted by the spirit of their maker. I don't know much of Drakonian history, only that a necromancer created life to fill the desert and survive on the only available food source – blood.

Another thought toys in my mind. How much of what I am seeing, hearing, and feeling does M'ra know? Is she aware I went to the Otherworld and collected a wraith? Do the boundaries of the Otherworld, a home for unsettled souls, shield me from the magic in her blood?

Why is her blood in you?

It reads my thoughts. This isn't any better than her spying on me.

I resent that and no. As a vampire she never truly died as her soul is intact. As long as I remain in you, she is blind to you.

That's a relief, I think sarcastically. Is it better she spy on me or the wraith read all my thoughts? Even she can't do that.

Watch what you think.

Tell me what I want to know.

The scythe first, it orders, its words form a heat that rushes through me like a ball of dragon fire.

The Abandoned Valley is a small area surrounded by lowlands. Nothing exists in it but cracked, hardened sand. Vampires don't even live here. There is nothing.

I don't have to project thoughts for it to find them. How do you know about Ryel?

It laughs wickedly. *Don't you remember? Your pain called for us. Your tears and agony brought us directly to you. We helped you keep your girlfriend from entering Tranquility.*

The memories flood me. I fought to keep her soul, unwilling to let Tranquility have it. Selfishly, I wasn't ready for her to leave this world and clung to all that was left of her. The shadows swarmed from every corner; darkness filled the space. It wasn't my magic, but my pain. It sang to them, begged them, and they answered. Guilt runs alongside the wraith inside me. They coexist.

Yes, you did this and now you'll find the scythe.

It leaves me without a choice, my soul anguishes as it forces me. My appendages no longer working for myself. They belong to the wraith. A wide crack spreads across the center of the basin, small fissures web off it like streams of sand.

The crack is largest marking the center of the Abandoned Valley, like an X marks the spot. Glancing down I see nothing but darkness. Creating a light, I drop it and watch as it falls deeper and deeper until it splashes. Its glow a dot in the underground brook.

I hold one foot over the edge, then the other, and plummet involuntarily into the abyss. Darkness swallows me whole, shame rises in my throat and I have no want to brighten my descent into the belly of Drakonia. Falling and falling until the crimson sky is engulfed by darkness.

A sticky liquid blankets my skin and clothing as I hit, my head falling below the surface, my feet unable to touch the bottom. Soon my head bobs above the surface. The wraith inside forcing me to follow the current. Blood drains from the top of my head. I blink and viscous commoner blood enters my eyes. I don't force it away from my eyes. I couldn't if I tried. The wraith is in control, taking my body for a ride. I swallow hard, my heartbeat drums in my ear. Through the blood draining into my eyes I spot my light several meters ahead, illuminating a dark corridor. The rushing water keeps it from coagulating which is why the blood cells and plasma are always mixed.

I allow the current to carry me, the sand walls smooth with weathering from the blood. I don't swim or fight. The wraith is in control. The water becomes shallow some distance from where I dropped. I don't know how far we've floated. My feet brush the bottom and my legs move without my consent as I stand, the blood rising no higher than my waist.

Step out of the blood and follow the cave deeper. Doing as the wraith commands, I follow the cave. It relinquishes some control and I move my own parts. I'm meters underground and have nowhere else to go. If I try to portal it will stop me. I remember the hunter in Lols. The one who put an arrow in my back and nearly killed me. Is this how she felt when I trapped her in an energy bubble and forced her to give up her weapon caches and sent her unwillingly to the arctic?

The brook continues one direction and I go another, following a carved, smooth path. Blood drips from my light. My shoes squish from the crimson coating, creating red shoeprints. The path leads to a small entrance. Crawling, I fit through it. On the other side it opens into a large cavern. In the center are decayed bones. Remnants of clothing, strings mostly, hang over the skeleton. *Now what?*

Beneath the bones is the scythe. It was buried with him and his body hidden here so no one could use it to create life from death again.

Digging through bones isn't on my to do list but I don't get a choice. I lift them up carefully. They are fragile and disgusting. Beneath them is a jade light. It shines as brightly as mine. The object has a curved head and jagged teeth. Its handle, solid jade, a green stone commonly found in Lols. The head made of a shiny metal such as silver.

Pick it up, the wraith orders.

I run a finger along the handle and see the teeth are embedded in the stone floor. It's smooth. The blade and teeth sharp as if the years haven't dulled them. I grip my hand around it, energy roils through me, cold like icicles. My body shivers from the inside out. Tightening my grip I clutch and pull. Energy explodes like a commoner bomb inside me and I'm forced backwards.

My head hitting the hardened cave wall, it detonates in pain and radiates through my body, shaking and rattling every bone. I don't know where it stops or starts. It's constant. My body twitches hysterically as frost pumps through my veins. My entire body is cold as ice, frozen daggers prickle my blood, chilling it to sub-zero.

The power of the magic the scythe holds is greater than any magic I've ever experienced. Objects are made to amplify magic, but this is different. It is connected to a source like none other, and more powerful than level 4. It's robust, authoritative, commanding, and stronger than the spell that created realm walkers. How is it possible?

I welcome the burning sensation as convulsions sweep over me. My body twitches and trembles as my throat closes. Air doesn't reach my airways. A lump the size of my fist forms at the back of my throat. I choke and gag until a black blob spews from my mouth, hitting the opposite wall.

The scythe falls from my hand to the ground, clanging like glass shattering. My head spins and my body drops.

5

The cavern grows dark, extinguishing my light. From the black moves a form, unable to make out much more than an outline, it grows. A light emerges behind it illuminating a man in a cloak. His face is covered by the hood. "There are three powerful forces: death, magic, and life," he says, his words rebounding from the walls of the cave.

I can't see his lips under the cloak and only imagine they are coming from the cloaked individual. "Magic works with life and death. In blood sacrifice life can be altered permanently as a pact but magic can create life through death. That is the strongest force."

He raises his cloak over his chest and drops it over his back. Dark marks like passport inkings mark his chest, arms, and neck. Most are lines with squiggles as if some ancient language, similar to old fae but one stands out above his waistline, a small lightning bolt just like Ryel's, and on his neck a scythe. Its shape exactly like the scythe of immortality, down to the teeth on the blade.

Other than him, the entire cave is black. I can't see the scythe or the wraith. He continues, "I was bestowed the power of life." As soon as the words leave his mouth he dissipates and in his spot is a blob. All colors radiate horizontally from it, rising into the air and disappearing in the darkness. The blob moves in and out as if sentient and breathing.

The voice continues, "Magic chooses the purest souls to do her bidding. You have been tainted by the touch of death. The council of divination will rise in you, but magic will reject you!"

The blob vanishes, replaced by a young girl and six others as they drink. It focused on the girl, blurring the others.

"One day," the image blurs and fades into darkness, "you will face magic and death will follow…" The voice fades to silence. My eyes open. I lay on the floor of the cave, my back against the wall. "You mustn't ever touch the scythe," echoes against the walls, bouncing back and forth until it disappears. Silence as quiet as death surrounds me.

Cyrus. I shake my head. *Cyrus.* It takes my mind a moment to register the voice in my head. As the thick fog clears, I realize it is Lamont.

What is it? I respond, trying to keep my head voice from quaking. Not much shakes me up, unsteadies me, but the cloaked man, this experience, the wraith has me on edge.

I've been trying you for hours. You OK?

No, yes. At this point I don't know. I am alive and the wraith is gone. *What is it?* I repeat, my head voice more clear, less wobbly.

His head voice clearly discombobulated as it treads on the words: *The hybrids have voted.*

How long have I been gone? I don't feel the wraith. I move my arms and legs. They do what I tell them. She's gone. I take heed of the cloaked man's words and open a portal. Matter does as I command it. I'm sure the wraith has fled. I portal the scythe to my inbetween world. I won't touch it. Thinking back to the moment I did, it was a compelling force. The wraith wanted me to touch it. *Why?*

The scythe is the embodiment of life. Did the cold vanquish it from my body? It used me as a host. *Why? What does it need and will it return?*

Realm Walker

Blood cakes my hands and clothing. I drop the clothes onto the floor to be burned and step into the shower. My inbetween world has grown. In my sorrow and desperation, In the dark days after Ryel's death I expanded my room, made myself a home. A place I'd never need to leave. A place for me and Ryel.

What happened? I see the man in my mind, hear his words and warning. *Who was he?* His talk of life and death, his words about creating life from death, and I know who he is…was. The father of vampires. None of the experience answers why M'ra has an interest in me.

I shout into the air, "I got the scythe! You owe me. What does she want, why me?" My words go unanswered.

I connect on the holocall with the hybrids and realm walkers. I study the faces as they blink in. The next phase beginning. When this started I didn't see this day and now don't care. Excitement doesn't consume me. The faces of the hybrids chosen as representatives do nothing to wrangle my thoughts or encourage words. I speak without awareness, my mouth on auto pilot, taken over by a part of my subconscious mind. I hear the words as if someone else is speaking.

From the corner of my eye Marilisa watches me with a thoughtful, untrusting gaze. A wreath like a tiara weaved with leaves, a golden seed from the serenity tree in the center, adorns her head. *Is that a gift from the elves for turning against me?*

What is her deal with the tree? She claims it is responsible for life as if it is immortal, a vessel in which magic and life work together to *create life out of death*. The man's words replay in my head. *Is he like the tree?* A legend claims the seed offers immortality, eternal life, but there is no proof.

After my experience I'd believe almost anything if there were evidence. My body still shaken and awkward. My arms and legs mine, my thoughts my own but changed. I'm an empty vessel, confused and weak. A walking, talking void, numb and disoriented. My thoughts scattered.

Why did it choose me and why do I feel so empty now that it's gone? Is that experience a clue to M'ra's obsession with me? Did she feel any of it?

Harvesters learn to capture souls and send them on to their afterlife, similarly elves learn to communicate with plants. It is central to who they are as a people. Culturally, each realm subspecies has skills that are at the heart of who and what they are and learned from infancy. *Can I learn to communicate with plants? Why am I thinking this?* I shake my head to rid the thoughts, but they are stuck like glue.

Is that tree important? The wraith duped me and I am dumber than the silly wreath on Marilisa's head. What the wraith wants is a secret. The meaning behind the vision a larger secret. I do understand sacrifice, death, and magic change life. Realm walkers are the embodiment of it. We call it level 4 magic, but is creating life through magic after death level 5?

The day Ryel died it was instinct for me to harvest her soul, not that I've ever harvested a soul before, but I was compelled, further compelled by my own need to keep her, stop her soul from leaving this plane. She is…was a hybrid. Her touch so real in the Otherworld. It lingers on my skin, her scent fills the air, eddying around me. She remains…because I can't let her go.

The rules don't apply to her. She belongs to Tranquility. *Will it return for her?* My heart clutches. No! The black shadows rose from below, gave me a boost to keep her grounded. Is her soul theirs now? Did I change her fate? Water wells in my eyes and I blink it away, aware I'm not alone. How much will they see in the call? No! My throat constricts. I opened a door and it can't be closed. I invited the wraith inside and it will return.

I surround her essence in energy. She is mine, not theirs, not belonging to Tranquility or the Otherworld. Mine. She glows deep violet and I wonder if I can communicate with her. My scattered thoughts coalesce. If Marilisa can teach me to

communicate with plants, can I use that skill
to connect with Ryel? I smile at Marilisa who
lowers her brows and narrows her eyes into
guarded half-moons, absorbing all the colors
of her surroundings. Sarcanthum blue,
Serenity gold, and silver dotted with lavender.

The meeting ends. I am both aware
and unaware of the conclusion. I see the faces
of the hybrids and realm walkers – all of
them. Each realm walker of my generation is
present. Anger flares. Days ago three betrayed
me, stopped me. Yet they are all here. Is that
the purpose of Ryel's death? A sacrifice
rallying cooperation. I still think Marilisa is a
spy for Aradia. She will bring their leader
word. Let her. Alone in my world, Lamont's
voice pops into my head. *Come to Sier. I have a
case of Canidan Hops.*

6

His words tempting. I haven't left my world other than my trip to the Otherworld and Drakonia since Ryel's murder. We sit on the thick steps of the old castle across from each other, our legs stretched in front of us. The steps are so wide the soles of our shoes don't touch. Even in the summer months the temperature never rises above 9°C. I call on energy and create a blanket of warmth around me.

Here I am in enemy territory. The dragons not ready to cooperate, meet halfway. Their stubborn nature unbecoming. My magic returned, I don't fear theirs. The Canidan Hops flow like honey down my throat.

Lamont runs a hand through his short, buzzed hair. "I've been thinking putting pressure on the realm leaders worked but not all are sold. The leaders we meet with tomorrow, if they agree, can pressure the other leaders, but in realms like Sier it's the dragons who need convincing. The realm is theirs. Laws don't pass without a majority of support from the dragons. Nothing changes without a majority of support. We need to apply pressure to the dragons, the fae, and the harvesters."

"How do you propose we do that?"

He shrugs. "I don't know. An idea is trying to form but I don't quite have it."

I stare at the realm sky, the moon and the stars shining and twinkling, but with my realm walker vision I see beyond that to the edge of the veil. As if the wraith is still on my shoulder, speaking slurs into my ears, an idea forms. It is not in me but I don't know if the idea is mine or hers. "The veils. If we put fissures in the veils, we show the people we mean business and demonstrate our strength as a whole."

He cocks his head to the side. "You're saying we weaken the veils?" he asks, his tone unsure. His thick brows furrowed.

"Exactly!"

He taps his fingers against the step for a moment. "Can we do that?"

My lips curl into a devious smile. Of course we can. I have taught them so much but not how to tear the realms apart. My intentions weren't to divide but connect. All has changed, diplomacy didn't work. It brought violence, killing Ryel, and now we return the sentiment. It's time to teach them the things I didn't. The things that will force the realm leaders. Things to bend their stubborn wills.

I make a hole in the matter at my fingertips, exposing the inbetween. The teal shade of the small fissure shines between us. Lamont's small, almond-shaped eyes grow in size and roundness. "How did you do that?"

"It's similar to portalling. We can mold and command energy and matter. Think of opening a portal, only steady it so it doesn't shift and move, then push it aside. Try it," I explain and encourage.

He squares his shoulders and puffs his bulky chest out, then wiggles his fingers.

"If you have to do all this every time it's going to be a long night," I tease.

He shoots me a cocky smile. "Fine, here we go." His eyes focus on the air. Our breath foggy in the tense air. He squeezes his eyes into tiny slivers and pulls with his fingers. Teeth grit and sweat forms on his brows as he pulls.

"Envision it," I coax.

With a grunt he pulls enough that a small teal hole appears. A smile sweeps over his face. Pride swells in his red cheeks.

I run my finger across the hole I created, and it vanishes. "Try it." It is almost a shame. All the effort he put into ripping the matter apart.

His brow quirks in question and he picks up his can of Canidan Hops, takes a swig, and sets it down on the step. Templing his fingers so the knuckles pop, he slides a hand over the hole he created and the teal swirling glow vanishes.

Movement catches the corner of my vision and I turn my head. A white dragon soars to my left and perches on a cliff meters below us. I don't stop the smile tugging at my lips. An idea blossoms in my mind. A dragon's hearing and vision is keen. I think the dragon could be a spy. Is probably a spy. I don't speak out loud as the dragon's hearing is acute enough to hear our every word, each inhale and exhale from our lungs. I use the comicay. With the chip blocking our conversation it won't hear us. *We are being watched. Follow me.*

His brows lower but he doesn't look. I descend the steps and run towards the veil between Thraves and Sier. It isn't far. It would be easier to portal, but I want the dragon to follow us. Through my realm walker vision I watch as the dragon lifts from the perch. Its wings spread wide as it soars towards us, keeping a safe distance like the hunters in Lols.

The terrain is rough as we push over crumbled rocks and permafrost. As realm walkers we are swift. We don't have extra physical strength but we are agile and quick. Closing in on the veil, the dragon swoops down releasing icy breath. It chills our backs. Icicles the size of swords hit the ground and break into chunks. I leap and dodge them, melt some, and keep going. Lamont's footfalls pound in my ears as he passes me. His legs and stride longer than mine.

He slows as he reaches the veil as if it can stop him as it does purebloods. Icicles drop and crash around him. They hit the veil and shatter like glass. *Keep going through the veil*, I urge. I don't see his face but imagine the uncertainty on it. Lips taut, brows drawn, and eyes question marks. He doesn't stop and goes right through it and I'm right behind him. I press a finger into the veil as I pass through and a long, wide fracture opens.

The dragon sails right through as if it doesn't notice it's on the other side…in Thraves. *This way*, I say through the comicay and veer to the right. My swift feet move in familiar territory. This is my land, my territory. I know it better than any other realm. I head toward the lower midlands. The dragon's icy breath on our backs, ice droplets melt as they touch my heat energy shield.

I see the rocky ledge ahead and pick up my pace. Lamont follows as we slide underneath. The dragon veers upwards at the last minute, frigid air turning the ledge glacier cold. It misses it and stops. Its wings push the air towards us. My realm walker vision watches as it turns. Its head cocks and suddenly it realizes it's not in Sier anymore. Its tail swishes, pushing a strong wind in our direction, blows loose rocks at our legs and feet and sends dirt towards our faces as it turns. Its massive wings move with precision as it returns to its own realm.

Lamont blinks the dirt from his eyes and rubs as he steps out from under the ledge. "How did it get through?"

"Fissures," I reply as I rest my back against the mountain.

7

I return to my inbetween, power returning to my essence, and mold the matter, creating a new space. My efforts to gain equality and using diplomacy to gain support, to ask for permission, morphs. It's not about that anymore. We don't need their permission. We can take what is ours and should, but to do that I have to convince the hybrids and realm walkers it's the only way.

I mold an office space large enough for all of us. No more joining together in holocalls. I show them what I can do and unite us under one roof, offering insight of my powers: realm walker powers. When it's finished it's large enough for everyone, with comfortable swiveling chairs and an eight-sided table representative of each middle realm and Provence.

It is a private, secure location. The doors open from a specific location in their respective realms and only the hybrids attending the meeting have knowledge of the location. The doors will vanish as soon as they enter, similar to the door I showed Ryel. The amusement and wonder on her face etched across my mind as if it was yesterday.

The hybrids stammer in wonder, tossing questions and statements. 'How did you do this?' 'Where are we?' 'What is this?'

I'm no longer confused, split between death and life, lost in grief, desperate and automatic. I am in control, authority and potential swelling in my chest and limbs. My brain clear of the earlier fog. I am ready to meet with the realm leaders. We are ready as the hybrids take their seats.

M'ra is the first to join the holocall, followed by Verboten, Canida, and Aradia. All watch me with skeptical eyes, except M'ra. I can't see her eyes through the silver veil but I know she watches. I feel it as if the drop of blood she offered works two ways.

"Thank you for meeting with us," I say, "and hearing our pleas. For centuries, hybrids have been outcasts, realm walkers have kept the peace between realms, done everything we were asked. We have fulfilled the position as a communication pawn between realms. It is time this changes. Time that we, with the hybrids, are given what is rightfully ours. We seek our own realm; Provence, and the ability to build our own government granting us the rights you take for granted and to form a larger government body to assist in realm relations, with diplomats from *each* of your realms."

The Aradian leader looks me square in my eye. Her colorful chair designed from the finest Aradian fabric. "We have a system that works. It isn't perfect," she tilts her head slightly upwards keeping her eyes on me, "but it works. How will the central government be an improvement?" She is testing me. I expect the push back.

It is the Verboten hybrid Malek who responds: "The central government would be a tribunal made from pureblood diplomats chosen by you to serve for the best interests of your realm. Each realm, including Provence, would be represented." His yellow plumage rests on his shoulder.

"And what of the diplomats from Provence?" the Canidan leader asks, his large frame shadowing the light-colored wall behind him. It is difficult to buckle down my disdain for him after what happened to Ryel. I want to wrap him in energy and strangle the life out of him. A plume of rage festers, itches at my soul. I don't only want him to suffer, but want to rip the flesh off the bones of Ryel's murderers' accomplices!

The Canidan hybrid responds, holding her head high, shoulders square: "We are the chosen diplomats for Provence."

The meeting continues as such, each leader voices their concerns and doubts. Questioning each and every thought put forward. They attempt unsuccessfully to poke holes into our concept. For every question a hybrid has a solid answer. They explain the design for the city, the mall with shops for every realm to share goods. No more day trading. With each leader's blowback tensions in the room rise, annoyance gnaws, attitudes stay cool but the heat boils.

I can take Provence if I want, seal the curtains and block them out, no day trading, nothing. They'd be locked in their own realms with no assistance from anyone but the older generation realm walkers. I don't play this card yet. "We are asking this as diplomats. Think on this and help bring in the other realm leaders. Tell them of the benefits."

M'ra appears to study us and narrows on me. Her gaze under the veil piercing my soul, prickling my thoughts like tiny needles in my brain. "How do you expect us to gain their confidence after a veil was torn open yesterday? A dragon flew into Thraves."

REALM WALKER

Of all leaders, I thought she was on our side. Not a single one said anything about the little experience, but of course she knows. As the leader of Drakonia, it borders Thraves, and the chief would communicate with her or her higher-ranking vampires.

The other hybrids turn to me, expressions saying more than the words stuck in their throats. Clearly they have no idea what she is talking about, or the realm leaders, who shoot confused and awkward stares directed at me.

Eight pairs of eyes glare at me expecting an explanation. I don't disappoint, feeding on the daggers of negative energy flowing through me. "It happened. I was with Lamont in Sier. We were minding our own business on the old palace steps when an ice dragon spotted us. It chased us, blowing frosty air and large icicles. It meant to kill us. We had no choice but to run towards the curtain and escape him, only we didn't until we reached a cliff overhang in Thraves. I don't know how it got through the veil or why it tried to kill us. This is an example of why we need our own realm."

"What did you do?" the Aradian leader snaps at me, her tone accusing.

"I did nothing wrong! It is the dragons you need to direct your rage at. It found a way through the veil, or they are weakening. They are hundreds of years old," I bite back, maintaining my false innocence.

The Verboten leader's yellow plumage spreads out like a fan behind her. "Then we have bigger problems. The veil needs to be mended."

"Do we? The realm walkers were created with the veils, surely they can mend them, but why should they if Sier and Thraves aren't willing to work with us, just as Navarin isn't?" the Navarin hybrid says, his expression firm and eyes cold. A not quite fae who has enough of something else to throw and adds fighting words to the boiling conversation. Tensions stretch across the holocall. The plume of rage climbs through my veins, beats with my heart, and feeds off the strain in their emotions and fear.

I interject: "What he says is correct. We can probably mend the veil if we work together. I think we'd be willing to make the attempt if Thraves, Navarin and Sier come around and see things our way." The realm leaders catch the subtle shape-up-or-you're-next threat in my tone.

"Our safety. What of our safety? If Cyrus and Lamont were chased through the veil, we aren't safe in our realms!" the Navarin hybrid says in a snippy fae tone.

"Hybrids are always welcome in Drakonia," M'ra offers.

Realm Walker

This is followed by the other leaders, some doing it with full conviction, others doing it because they want to one up M'ra. It is a half-hearted attempt to show they are on our side, driven by their own insecurities and dread. They don't want to be next.

The verboten hybrid presses his lower arms to the table and leans in. "This is one more reason why we need our own realm. If we aren't safe in our home realms, then are we safe anywhere? Provence should be ours."

The rising darkness inside me simmers and cools to the shadows of my soul, where it waits.

The call ends with realm leaders doing as we ask. They will speak to the Navarin fae queen, Supreme Dragon, and Thraves' Chief. The man who sent me to Lols because I don't play by the rules. The irony takes hold of my lips and they curl at the edges.

The hybrids play it off well. Without the words spoken, they know I am somehow responsible, or at least it is in the back of their minds, chewing on their subconscious. They ask the most logical question: 'Can other veils be weakened?'

My smile swells. It is the first true happiness I've felt since my last peaceful seconds with Ryel.

8

After the meeting, I do something I haven't done in many months: I portal to my parents' home. My goal is to see my father, who is in charge of those who are offered a second life as a vampire. Surely he understands something about their customs.

My mom, fortunately, isn't home. My dad tugs on shoes as he gets ready for work. Teal portal light dissipates in the doorway of the bedroom. He turns to me, love in his swirling eyes. "Cyrus. You've come home."

The man who isn't my biological father but loves me like his own child.

Compassion and tenderness burst from him and glow like an Aradian sarcanthum flower. "No, I've come to see you."

He adjusts the collar on his shirt below the bulk of his beard then walks to me and places his hands against my upper arms. "What can I do for you?"

I pull the comicay off and stuff it into my pocket. He follows my lead. His comicay lacks the chip hybrids and realm walkers use to communicate in private. "What do you know about how vampires were made?"

His bushy manicured brows twist in confusion. It isn't what he expected. "Nothing more than anyone. They are very secretive about their making."

I don't want to tell him about the scythe in case he and my mother are ever questioned. Maintaining his innocence is important. The chief mustn't know of my visit or his life may be in danger, and M'ra doesn't need to know more than she already does. "Is there a place I can find those answers?"

He taps his foot nervously. "You are seeking dangerous knowledge."

"I know and understand, but you know something." The tell is his nervous foot.

"I might." He takes a deep breath as if what he has to say might be his last words. "It is said that Blood Fountain, in the center of the minister's palace on the bottom floor, opens to an underground staircase holding many secrets." He kisses my forehead. "Be safe."

For an instant I soak in his love. It drips over my heart like honey. The shadows in my soul scurry like vermin. I don't feel them, but I know they are there, waiting. I fold my arms around him and rest my head against his shoulder long enough to smell his aftershave.

The tower is heavily guarded. I need a distraction. I mull it over as I relax in the trella provided by the Aradian leader. A trella is their word for house. I accepted the offer to maintain my innocence. Appearances are everything, or my manipulation efforts are nothing. I don't plan on staying long, only long enough. It isn't luxury, but homey, with couch cushions soft and plump enough to sleep on, tapestries of Aradia hang on the walls, and a fire roars in the hearth. It will do.

A tap on the door catches my attention. I open the door and Marilisa stands on the other side, the colors of the forest reflected in her hair and eyes. She is part of the reason I accepted. Her beautiful features marred with worry and concern as she pushes her way in without waiting for an invitation. I turn and watch as she leans into the other doorways. It's like she's checking to make sure we are alone.

I close the door. "I know you haven't come here to be sure I'm safe or comfortable."

She whips around, her long braid flowing with the movement and slapping against her back as it settles. "You have to stop!"

I laugh. "You think I can stop this? What's done is done."

"You started it! Find a way," she demands. Her exasperation flares.

"Even if I could, why would I want to?" I say, leaning against the wall.

She folds her arms across her chest and sighs audibly. "Serenity is shrinking at a faster rate than ever."

The tree again. I hold my arms out. "A tree. That's why this should stop. What does your realm leader say to this?"

Her hazel eyes narrow into half slits. "She thinks it'll start growing again once we convince the other leaders to get on board."

"But you don't agree."

She drops onto the arm rest of a fluffy chair. "No. Serenity used to take up half the realm, her leaves offering shade over the moat surrounding her, now she is only a fraction of that."

I take a seat on the chair and look upwards, meeting her gaze, sizing my next words and bathing in the sparks of her anger. If I want to get in with her, I need to play her games. "I don't understand Elfin customs," I catch the end of her braid and swing it over her shoulder, "but if you can teach me to talk with plants maybe we can find a solution."

Distrust radiates from her eyes. She smooths the braid, her hand lingering at the end, and twists the loose hairs. "How can that solve anything?"

She isn't an easy one, uptight, stubborn, yet attractive with her petite curves and chiseled features. "The trees have secrets to tell. If they trust me, maybe they tell. Maybe that same magic can be used to find a better solution."

She shoots to her feet and marches to the door. Swinging it wide she steps outside. After a couple minutes she says, "Are you coming?"

I walk alongside her as she leads us into dense woods. I find it fascinating how plants move for her. They part and lift their branches so she can walk beneath. They don't do the same for me and I tuck and weave to avoid scratches.

The magic lesson involves the manipulation of sound. We listen to the silence, until chatter fills the void. It is a different chatter than listening to others speak, a higher frequency. There can be many uses for this. At this point the plants aren't talking to me, but I hear them and can easily filter through the conversations. They discuss hybrids and realms and something else.

'The veil is weak, you know Sier was torn open.'

'I hear it can be fixed.'

'Impossible, they were created before we were seedlings.'

'Speak for yourself.'

Huffs, curiosity, and discontent filter in their words. An idea itches at me and a plan forms.

9

"What are you?" a female Lols vampire seethes, holding in the pain from the wolf blood-soaked arrow in her thigh.

In order to trap a vampire, I needed immobilizing weapons. CIU had those in evidence lock up. I portalled in and grabbed a wolf blood-soaked arrow that I brought back from my London trip a year ago. Blood trickles from the vampire's thigh. Commoner hybrid lycan blood is weaker than pureblooded Canidan. It won't die, at least not right away, but it will bleed and the odor of vampire blood is sure to bring in wolves.

I transformed into one of the hunters I'd met in London as a clever disguise. "A hunter," I reply, holding the vampire in an energy web caused by the dead. A gateway of sorts that spirits use to travel in Lols. They are everywhere but most commonly in cemeteries, where the energy of the dead gathers. The vampire can't see it, nor does it appear to sense it, making it all that much easier to trap it inside. I hold it with my energy.

She grits her teeth. The wolf blood burning, black lines form around the arrowhead. The wound will worsen, and her skin will rot. "The vampires will kill you!" she threatens in shortened breaths.

An empty threat. "How is it you walk in the sun?" It is a cloudy winter day, the skies gray, but I'd tracked her for days as she walked under full sunlight. Curious. I'd never known a vampire able to do that.

She struggles against the force of energy holding her captive and the agonizing pain in her thigh. Her nose and face pinch when she hears the thunder of wolf paws pounding the dirt. It is a beautiful sound. Holding the gateway open, I portal out of sight. My plan isn't to kill the vampire. She's bait.

I watch from a distance as the wolves descend on her. They circle in their commoner forms, eyes glowing. Snouts form, teeth sharpen, ears perk, and claws extend as they partially shift. These wolves are different than pureblood lycans. Their hybrid blood washed out. Drool hangs from their jowls as their thirst to kill the vampire is primordial. Vampires and wolves, no matter what realm, are enemies.

The wolves close in. The vampire rotates in agony. I let go of my energy field holding the vampire in place but keep my hold on the gateway. "You don't want to do this," the vampire says.

"You're in our territory," a male wolf snarls as it stalks closer, studying the awkward situation. Its ears and snout covered in gray fur. "Hunters?"

"One that calls itself a hunter, but it has magic and stuck me with this arrow."

The wolf roars in laughter. "A hunter did this and where is it?"

"It chased me here and vanished."

"Hunters don't vanish," he says.

Another walks to his side, tilting its brown furry head sideways as it examines the vampire in the precarious situation. It sniffs. "And they don't have magic."

The first one moves around the vampire. "And they don't wound. They kill. The wolf blood in the arrowhead is getting into your head."

I scoop the wolves into my tractor beam of energy and force them into the gateway, releasing the injured vampire. They dangle for a moment as I bend the gateway, sending them to Drakonia. It happens so quick the wolves don't have time to protest as they vanish. A sense of accomplishment settles in my bones. They aren't the guilty lycans that killed Ryel, but my hate extends to all wolves.

The diversion works and the guards thin as the lycan intrusion quickly catches their attention. I portal into the bottom floor of the high tower. The memory of standing here with Ryel's lifeless body in my arms is almost too much to bear. I pause, close my eyes, and concentrate on the murk hiding in the shadows of my soul. I use it as a crutch to mask the ache in my heart.

I open my eyes and find the fountain. It is where my father said. Beneath it is the room. His information is correct. Its contents are fuzzy. The energy in the room agitates my vision. The space isn't large.

In order for the gateway to work, I made a thin fissure in the veil of Provence, extending to Canida and Drakonia. Since they aren't connecting realms, Provence was the only option as it connects every realm.

Crimson blood flows from an open mouth of the fountain into a pool below, recycled into the mouth again. I don't have much time as I move around the fountain. There's a stone lip telling me it moves. I command energy and attempt to push it out of the way. It doesn't budge so I attempt to portal without success.

I search the base of the fountain for anything out of place, something to press or a lever to pull. A flaw even, but there's nothing. My time is growing shorter. They'll return soon. I focus on the fuzzy room. Strong magic wards it, meaning whatever is down there is valuable.

I search the fountain room. Looking through the walls is nothing but beams and stuffing, however, the crown molding is shallow in one area. I lift myself from the ground to the high ceiling and stick my hand through the molding. A neat realm walker trick.

My hand brushes a metal object. It fills the small space in the molding. I push it out with a fingernail and clutch it with my hand. It isn't as small as I thought and fills my entire palm. It's weighty, made from a heavy metal. A key, I think. A red stone similar to the one in the minister's ring in the top with two prongs beneath. My instinct says it fits the mouth of the fountain and where the blood flows from is the keyhole.

Voices filter into my head and I crunch my body into a tight ball in the corner of the ceiling. A male vampire with short, chestnut-colored hair enters the room and stops at the fountain. Depressing his comicay, he holds a private brain-to-brain conversation I can't hear. His eyes lift and head tilts as he stares at the ceiling. My body tenses, breathing increases, and my heart pumps as I prepare to slide along the molding.

10

I let out a long breath when the vampire moves and lower myself to the ground. I stuff the key into the mouth of the fountain. Sticky blood courses over my hand and wrist. Standing on the edge of the fountain to reach the mouth, it jolts. My body sways forward. I put my arms out to balance myself when it jolts again and I sway backward. Stumbling on the ledge of the fountain, I let my body fall to the floor. I drop to the tile, landing on my tailbone. A sharp pain moves up my spine and jars my neck as I hit the floor. I clutch the key and stand unsteadily.

REALM WALKER

I'm still alone and limp to the stone steps into the dark belly below. It swallows me, surrounding me like a glove. The fountain slides into place and sconces illuminate on the wall uncovering more and more steps, winding steps dropping into the depths of Drakonia. One step at a time, I move forward, my tailbone throbbing with each step. I come to a bend. The steps spill into a room. It's larger than the fountain and round. Energy like icicles stings my flesh from the inside, like glacial bugs trapped under it. They crawl inside me and escalate with each anguished step.

Its brick-and-mortar walls built to hide their secrets and warded with heavy magic. It's not fae, but something different… alien to me. When my feet hit the dirt floor the glacial bugs scatter and power like the plasma in every star rushes through my veins. It intensifies, radiating through my orifices until I think my body will burst, then scatters like the bugs, dissipating into the room.

Scrolls and more scrolls, covered with layers of dust several centimeters thick, are stacked against the walls. No one's been down here for commoner centuries. I dare to pick up a scroll. Dust falls like water, trickling to the floor I realize isn't dirt. It's dust. I have the key to the secrets of the vampires, each filthy scroll of their past, their maker. The one whose bones they hid under the Abandoned

Desert. Most of all, I have the scythe of immortality. It is no longer about M'ra's interest in me. I own their dirty secrets.

I lay the key at my feet and open the scroll. Dust fills the air and chokes me. I cough several times, spewing it from my lungs. It scratches like glass then subsides. I pull my shirt over my nose and study the writing. Old fae – their native tongue. Used today for spellcasting. The lines are thicker, the swirls not as pronounced as the old fae I've read, but I do recognize it. The man in my vision – he had markings exactly matching the scrolls. Did the fae create vampires?

The fae don't mark their skin. I'm fluent in Old Fae and the differences between this and my experiences with old fae make the scrolls difficult to read, but not impossible. Am I overthinking it? Maybe the writer used a heavy hand, but the more I look the surer I am it is distinctly another language. I unroll more scrolls and study the print. The differences popping the more I look. I'm sure it's another language, a similar language made by a similar people, surely old fae hasn't changed this much over time. No, it hasn't. They are proud and use it today because it is their tongue.

I don't have time to study each one, nor can I take them all. I collect a handful and tuck them under my arm. |Dust tickles my flesh and drops to the floor.

Realm Walker

I hear footfalls and muffled voices above me. I tune into my realm walker senses but they can't see past the bricks above my head, nor can I hear their speech clearly. The alien magic blocks my senses and abilities.

A red glow grabs my attention. The key, the red stone burning like a flame. Voices murmur around the room. I spin in one direction then another, but I am alone except for the key. *Pick it up,* a voice calls to me. The last time I'd listened to a voice a wraith hijacked my body and ice shot through my core. *Is it here?* "Show yourself!" I call.

Through the red light, I watch the darkness in the corners of the room for shadows, expecting them to coil around me, but none do. A wraith outside the Otherworld can't easily take a physical form and when I touched the scythe it forced her out of me. I am alone.

I attempt a portal. It fails. I'm not surprised, since my realm walker senses don't work either. Another reason I know these scrolls aren't fae. Merla was a sea fae. It was a spell she concocted that created realm walkers. We are made with magic commanded by fae.

I press my hands against the wall to search for a weakness in the magic and am thrown backwards into the opposite wall. Scrolls drop over my feet as my back smashes the wall, ripples of agonizing pain radiate through my joints.

Impossible! My anger at the fae or fae-like people who built this room sparks, flames catching. The heat moves through my limbs and I gather my strength, ready to blow the room apart, the entire building if needed.

Stop! The key will guide you, the voice calls. My gaze drifts to the key, red light spilling over the room. Magic has failed me. In this room, I am no more than a commoner. I reach for the key and squeeze my eyes shut as if that will stop the pain I know is coming.

I open an eye when nothing happens. The red light no longer shines over the room but from a beam against the wall. It forks a couple centimeters. A distance equal to the prongs in the key.

The route I came was never the way out. I match the prongs in the key to the beams of light and the bricks dissolve. Two scrolls perched against the wall next to the door drop onto my feet and roll. I collect them under my arm with the others and take one last glance at the room. The steps are gone, replaced with a brick wall.

I step forward into the dark hall. No lights automatically illuminate as they did when I followed the stairs into the room. I bring my other foot forward and nothing happens. No glacial bugs or energy plastering me to a wall. Nothing. The key still bright in my palm I use its light, holding it in front of me.

The corridor twists and turns like a maze. The air grows stuffy, making my head light, lost beneath the realm of death. How did my father even hear of this place? A guess, whispers from the dead? When vampires are given a second life, do spirits whisper of their past? Do particles of magic leave breadcrumbs? My father certainly isn't high enough ranking to be told of the room or the scrolls. I wonder at this point if the minister even knows.

My breathing labors the further I go. The air thickening. I rest my back against the wall and suck in a deep breath and release. I have to get out. Surrounded by brick walls with no magic I'm a mouse in a labyrinth with no idea what is waiting at the next bend.

I force myself up and onward. Tell myself I have to keep moving. Each turn, each corridor identical to the last. No forks, no choices. One tunnel after another. "You spoke to me before, speak again. How do I get out of here?" I ask the key.

Its light shines around the bend, flashing against the brick walls. "How do I get out of here!" I scream at the key and thrust it against the wall in my anger. It drops with a clank, echoing through the passages, then stops suddenly. Echoes don't die like that. They keep bouncing. The exit is close.

With a second wind I collect the key and continue, struggling with each breath, each step I take. My feet heavy and legs like jelly. *Another step. You can do it. Almost there.* I sweet talk my mind, coax it to continue until finally I reach a room, similar to the other room. It is round, but lacks any scrolls. Instead, in the center is a pillar, approximately a meter high. In the center are two holes that match the width of the prongs.

I don't think. I don't care. I decide to take my chances. If death wants me, I'm right here. I want out and push the key into the holes. The light extinguishes and bricks vanish, exposing a hidden stairway. It grinds like metal teeth rubbing against one another. Light pours through the widening slit. I pull the weighty key out of the wall and take the steps two at a time. I'd do three if my legs were long enough. The floor closes over my head. I hurry my pace and make the final step, sliding my body through the slender gap. It closes as I pull my arm to my side and suck in a deep breath.

REALM WALKER

11

The glowing stalactites shining from the cave ceiling and stalagmites poking from the solid floor are the most welcome sight. I'm not in Drakonia anymore but Thraves. I close my eyes, absorbing the sensation of home. I know Thraves better than anywhere. It is my home realm, one that has rejected me. My vision tells me where I am and I smile wide. My magic is back, no longer blocked by whatever alien magic was in the corridor and rooms.

I create a portal and send the scrolls and key into my inbetween world and send myself to Aradia. A single light on in the trella, someone is there. I push the door open, ready for a shower, when Lamont comes out of nowhere, grabs my shirt collar and pins me to the wall. He has many dragon attributes and superior physical strength is one of them.

"Where have you been?" His hazel eyes flash under the lights and his nose turns up as he lets go of me. "You stink!'

You would too. "Taking a shower." I pull my shirt off.

"No. Where have you been? I've tried to contact you. I got nothing. You were gone. Gone, gone."

Was I? Did that mean M'ra couldn't sense me either? There was no magic down there, not familiar magic. "I was in Lols."

"Lols? Why?" He steps in front of me, blocking me, his arms folded across his chest. He is a big guy but can't stop me. I won't harm him but I might use energy to push him gently aside.

"Is this an inquiry? You said I stink. I need a shower." I sidestep him, no magic, and he matches it, blocking my path. "Have I done something?"

"There's another fissure in a veil between Canida and Drakonia. It's large, extending all the way through Provence. I know you made that one between Sier and Thraves. Did you do it?"

I should have showered in my world. "I was in Lols. I took my comicay off. I didn't want to be found."

"They got Hackey." He steps out of my way.

"What?"

"Hackey. They got him. A vampire was injured and the minister is out for heads. Namely ours. Canida collected Hackey and brought him in." The remorse in his voice settles on me.

Why should I worry about Hackey? If it wasn't for him, Marilisa, and Jine I'd have had my revenge for Ryel's death. I grab his shoulders. "He can save himself. If we do it, we look guilty and it goes bad for us and the hybrids."

"I know. I've ran it through my head but we're next. They know. You showed your power and now none of us are safe."

Showed my power. Ryel showed her power first, shifting in Provence and killing her lycan murderer. I see through him. He's more worried about himself. Realm walkers don't turn on each other. "We give them something else to focus on." I collect my shirt from the back of the chair and thrust it over my shoulder, my body achier than I realize from all the slamming and toxic magic. Warm water washes off the grime and filth from the tunnel and spirals down the drain. We'll give them a distraction, I think as I pull fresh pants over my throbbing legs. More fissures in the veils.

While the realms are busy figuring out why and how they got there, I can figure out what to do with the scythe and the scrolls. If we keep the realms busy I can do what I please. It is possible to cause more cracks in the veil.

The one between Drakonia and Canida would be easy to open completely between all seven realms, as it is a pole where they all came together, like Provence, except the land isn't… That's it. I'll stretch the area between the realms at that pole and create a place only hybrids and realm walkers can go. It will take at least two passports to get in.

A smile slides over my face. I slip a fresh shirt on then stroll into the main room, my wet hair unbrushed and dripping onto my back. I shake my head and each strand falls into place. Lamont sits on the couch, a grumpy, annoyed expression on his face. Standing by the door are two exoilers – elfin police. "Have you come here to protect us?" I ask.

The shorter elf has a full quiver of arrows strapped to his back and braids falling over his shoulder. He narrows his vibrant blue eyes. "No. We are taking you in for questioning."

His tone unmistakably serious in the extreme, I feel the need to push him. "Have you talked with the Vizier?" That is Aradia's leader. The commander of the government.

"We need you both to come with us," the other exoiler commands. Her voice harsher and face lacking any expression.

I can't get a rise out of either of them. Lamont stays quiet, skulking at me as his eyes narrow into tiny slits. *We can get out at any time. If we run, we look guilty,* I think to him through our hacked comicays.

He nods and stands as if accepting a horrible fate. It isn't that bad. I can create an all-new Provence, but for now they want to talk to us. "Is this about Provence?" I ask, playing dumb.

The female exoiler, her bun pulling the skin in her cheeks taut, making her even less attractive. Her large, pointed ears stand out from her head like small wings. She pulls the door open. Lamont and I step out. The sarcanthum flowers glow as blue as an elf's eyes.

12

The exoilers leave us in the custody of two higher ranking officials who sit us down in an office. It isn't horrible. I wonder if this is how Canida is treating Hackey. A female sits behind a desk. One leg folded over the other, her hands chin level, one rubbing the back of the other.

Her face a cacophony of disappointment. She studies us for a long minute before finally speaking. "There's been a tragedy. It seems the veil between all the realms at the west pole has been breached. What can you tell us about that?"

"Us? How could we possibly have anything to do with that?" Lamont asks, his tone convincing as he really knows nothing, only suspects.

"We've seen your power." Her eyes stare into mine. "The veil between Sier and Thraves cracked as the two of you raced through it?"

She says it as proof I did it. "We had nothing to do with that. We were trying to get to Thraves to be safe from the dragon. It was a shock when it followed us and that's why we are staying in Aradia. Your Vizier was kind enough to provide a refuge for us, but I no longer feel safe here."

She glances away from me and focuses on Lamont. "And you?"

"Maybe we can help. We can try and mend the veil."

She chuckles for an instant then her lips pinch. "We have that taken care of."

Oh. Yes, our parents. I can take care of that from where I sit. I think. I weakened the veils in anger when Ryel...I focus on the realms, each veil, seam, and curtain. The steady beat of the realms pumps in unison with mine. One heartbeat, steady and sure. I hold my half smile and collect energy in the palms of my hands, holding them steady beneath the desk and send it outward toward the poles. It winds through the realms like a heat-seeking commoner missile. "Then why do you need us?"

She ignores my question and taps a finger against the back of her hand. With a twist of her lips she stands and places her hands on the desk. "Wait here."

The energy beam pushes against the parent generation as they try to mend the veil. The more they try the more energy I push against them. The invisible barrier strains as my magic counters theirs. It thins and twists, bending and bending until it snaps. Ripples bounce through it from one end to the next, creating many fissures. Not large like the others but present. My work is done.

She knows, Lamont's voice speaks into my head.

No, she doesn't. She's hoping we'll speak, give away our guilt. That's why she left. She's probably listening right now but all she hears is our breathing. I pick up the framed picture on her desk. A couple of elfin children I assume are hers. I put it back and stand, stretching my achy legs. I move around the small office. My tail bone throbs and neck pinches with each step.

I think M'ra's blood has worked its way through my system or the pain wouldn't be this intense and I'd be in Drakonia and not here in a stuffy room with exoilers. It means the cord is severed.

REALM WALKER

A vampire was injured? Bit? A Drakonian vampire. I don't think the hybrid Lols' bite is enough to kill a true Drakonian vampire. I left the Lols bait in Lols. What do they want with Hackey? A tingle of something almost foreign slips into my heart, stabbing at the blackness that scatters – remorse. He was a friend until he betrayed me. I harden my shield, welcome the shadows to return. Hackey doesn't deserve my remorse or empathy. He is a realm walker. The unfamiliar feeling returns.

I think of something else. I have ancient scrolls. Do they tell blood secrets? Secrets that create life from the scythe in my possession. Is there a way to test blood without a vampire? I know a couple hybrid CIU. They never tested my blood after the transfusion when M'ra snuck hers in, but I don't doubt their skills. CIU has been solving realm crimes for decades. The vampire in Lols is immune to daylight. How is that possible? Vampires without knowledge of Drakonia? It raises many questions and I have little patience for this foolishness. However, I do have hybrid legal friends.

I wait patiently on the outside, steaming on the inside. On the desk, next to the picture, is a clock. I set a limit on how long I'll wait until I contact Dygal, a hybrid Aradian lawyer who helped write our proposed laws and legal system.

The clock ticks and the door opens. "You are free to go," the elf says, her blue eyes flashing in distrust. My handywork from inside this room showed our parents can't fix what's broken. They aren't strong enough. The leaders will begin to distrust them and we are innocent. There's no way we possibly did anything from the inside of this room. I don't think they trust as at all but we are innocent…for now.

Lamont wastes no time standing and stepping into the hall, his shoulder brushing the ends of her hair. They fly up in static shock. I pause in the doorway. "You've made a wise choice. May I ask why your change of heart?"

"No, leave before minds are changed."

OK, OK, wouldn't want to ruffle any feathers.

Lamont's scruffy voice filters into my head. *I felt the ripple of energy through the veils in my core. Did you?*

Yes. It throws the blame off us.

Lamont's anger turns my skin into a hotbed of needle pricks. The pain centers my thoughts. He vanishes in a flash of teal before exiting the building. I inhale, the sour taste of anger fills my lungs.

Since Ryel's death and the invasion of the wraith I'm different, my connection to magic is changing, strife encourages it, coaxes it. It's thicker and pulpy. I've always been more aware than other realm walkers and learned at a very young age how to control the gift provided with the realm walker curse, but today, in that office, I didn't have to touch the matter to make it move, to break it.

Am I stronger because I bear the weight of double realm walker magic? Is that why the wraith possessed me in the first place? It never answered my question or told why it wanted me to find the scythe. Did it think I could return her to her human form? Maybe it isn't the wraith at all but the scythe and remnants of its magic remaining inside me.

I portal in my own teal flash.

13

The light dissolves. Lamont is standing in the middle room of the trella, his thick chest heaving with each breath. Shoulders rising and falling. He turns to me. "I can't believe you! I'm here because of you. My family isn't safe with me there and now they probably aren't safe with me here! You have no concern or empathy for anyone else but you! Always you!" he says, his voice rising with each word.

I've never seen him like this. Didn't know this side of him existed. "I have family too. My mom and dad are in Thraves. They're in as much danger as yours!" I hurl the words at him.

His fists ball and a whirl of energy smashes into my chest, lifting me off my feet and driving me backwards into the wall. My breath expels and the picture to my right crashes to the floor, shattering into tiny, sharp pieces that scratch my pants, tearing holes and poking into my legs. I'm impressed with his strength.

He marches at me, arms lifted slightly at his sides. My lungs labor for each breath and I don't have the chance to defend myself before busy, nippy energy encapsulates me. Lamont's hand moves from his side in front of his face and I slide upwards with it. He controls me like a puppet. "Everything is going haywire and you just keep…doing…all the…things that make it worse. Nothing you do makes it better. They'll go after our parents. Did you even give a moment's pause to consider that?" His brain struggles to put the words together.

My airways are breathing now. Not normal, but improved. The power behind the energy blast was incredible. I admire it. Admire his anger and blooming strength. It was always in him. "Yes," I say in a strangled voice. "I'm leaving here…" I pause and suck in as much air as my thrashed lungs will hold. "We aren't safe. We have to demand they give us Provence. They have no choice now." I pause for another lungful. "Don't you see? No one is safe, not you, not me, not our families, not even Marilisa, but we can mend the veils. We can use that."

The angry energy surrounding my body doesn't let up and I don't fight it. "You don't even hear yourself." He shakes his head. "I thought we were friends. You have no friends. When I told you about Hackey, you shrugged it off. No big, who cares, he's the lycan realm walker. I'm going to get him and I don't need you!"

His words slice the sliver left of my heart. The consuming energy dissipates and I slide down the wall, landing on the same pointed fragments of the picture and my already injured tailbone. It jars, and ripples of sharp pain move up my spine and neck.

He stomps away toward his room shouting, "I'm not returning!"

The door bursts open and Marilisa's petite frame seems to tower in the doorway. Her eyes flashing pools of red heat. She doesn't wait to be invited, slamming the door behind her. The tapestries on the wall rattle and slant sideways.

Hands at her sides, her chest heaving in and out, pulsing with the rhythm of her flaming eyes. "The tree is dying, veils are ripping, wolves are invading Drakonia, tensions are rising and the lycans are holding Hackey!" She thrusts an arm with a pointed finger in the direction of Canida. "And the two of you are—" Her soliloquy stops cold as she studies my precarious position on the floor and Lamont's scowl. He looks like fire might explode from his mouth at any moment, bringing the entire trella to a pile of singed dust.

"I'm going to get Hackey. You coming?" he asks her.

"Absolutely!"

My lungs are breathing normally now and I pull myself up. "Not alone," I say.

Both glare at me. I'm really glad neither breathes fire. Lamont walks past me, ignoring my presence, and opens the door. The sarcanthum flowers shine bright and solaflies blink in and out of the flora.

We blink through teal portals into the center of the legal capitol of Canida. It's not like Johnston's Pass with cozy wood structures and a view of Sier's highlands. Wide steps made for large lycan feet ascend to tall brick buildings reaching into the sky. Lights brighten the streets, and the prairies Canida is famous for don't exist in the metropolis.

I contact the lawyer through our comicay. His response is quick. *I'm on it. Paperwork is done and they're bringing him out now. Don't do anything hotheaded.* His head voice is calm and all business.

I can't promise the boiling cauldrons with me won't try something stupid but I'm gentle as a Navarin seabreeze, mostly because every part of my body, including parts I wasn't aware of, ache and burn. In the past week I've been inhabited by a wraith and icy magic from the scythe, beaten, battered, and bruised.

The lawyer's voice speaks in my head. This time it's not settled but shaken and almost condemning. *They're accusing him of murdering three lycans. The three you tried to kill in Provence, but there's no bodies.*

This stabs me straight in the heart. I've hated on Marilisa, Hackey, and Jine for their betrayal yet skulked in my room instead of enacting my vengeance. Someone else has stolen that glory and satisfaction of watching them squirm and beg as they die an agonizing death.

Marilisa taps a foot, arms folded across her chest, lips drawn so taut small lines cut into them. "What did he say?"

"That he's got it under control and not to do anything hot-headed."

Lamont lets out: "Pfff…you not do anything hot-headed." He shakes his head and paces, walking past Marilisa then back.

Seconds stretch into centuries as we wait at the legal square. Marilisa's foot tapping like a drumstick, back to me, and Lamont paces six large steps forward, turns on his heel and six steps back. Lycan lawyers scuttle past us and I count the number of pedestrians.

Marilisa's hair reflects silver from the light of the moon, with shimmers of pink and blue from the stars blinking in the darkness. I shift my gaze to the steps and will my mind not to watch them.

Several more minutes pass and I see Hackey and the lawyer descending the steps. My aching body and the palpable tension, I'm overjoyed when they approach. The hybrid lawyer wears a dark suit, his shoes shiny as the stars. White light reflects from them with each step.

Lamont stops his pacing but Marilisa's foot continues to pummel the ground beneath it. "He can go home for now but is expected in court on Day 1." In Lols that would be a Monday. "The lack of bodies won't keep him safe in the current political climate. I need evidence."

"I know people in Thraves," I say.

Hackey doesn't say a word until after the lawyer leaves. Lamont and Marilisa smother him with conversation and she wraps her arms in a hug around him. A twinge of emotion pings in my dead heart. I lost Ryel and have been to the Otherworld and back, my body thrashed, and I got anger not hugs. Jealousy. The annoying pang is jealousy.

I wait, contacting my connections at CIU. I know the purebloods won't lift a finger to help him but the few hybrids will.

Hackey steps beside me and leans to my ear. "You'll find what you want beneath Provence. There are tunnels."

My brows lower in surprise. "You—"

He cuts me off quick, holding up his hands. Silver bands wrap his wrists. "I can't leave Canida and they took my comicay." I don't think the silver will hold him.

Shock and disbelief tremor inside me and settle comfortably into respect. He didn't kill them, but put them somewhere no one but a realm walker can find them. It's clever and devious, but the comicays will be a problem. I don't know how long we have before they find the chip. Our communication is compromised.

14

Preston's voice isn't one I expect to hear in my head. My true father, he's aided me in the past but will he still? I don't trust him any more than my mother. *The minister would like to speak with you.*

I have no want to see M'ra but, to keep relations smooth, I agree. I leave the meeting and portal to the tower. Memories of the previous day and wandering in the labyrinth for hours with no magic sends a ripple of shivers over my spine. I don't portal to the lobby, too many memories. I choose the hall outside her office on the highest floor of the tower.

The same guards, the pint-sized deadly force female vampire and the hulking broad-chested male wide as the door. He opens the door when I approach, doesn't ask any questions. They are expecting me.

I glance to the window. She's not there waiting. Through the tint I see the light sands, crimson sky, and Drakonia's signature mark – Blood River. The sand sparkles like tiny glass shards. A teal light flashes behind me. I turn as it dissolves around M'ra, the minister of Drakonia. The aged vampire whose blood ran through my veins saving my life and giving her the ability to feel my emotions. A maroon veil covers her face. One of many in her large collection. I'm positive they have their own closet. She is a tiny shell of a woman.

I don't say anything and wait as she strolls to the chair and sits. "The veils are weakening, a large fissure spreads from Canida to Drakonia. I need your help in mending it."

No mention of the wolves or injured vampire. They aren't lycans and only appear to partially shift. Lycans shift all the way. Their human forms changing into furry, ferocious wolves. *Is this a game?* "I can't do it alone."

"I think you can," she says as if she knows.

This is where I want them. In an uncomfortable enough spot to force their hand. We mend the veils, the realm leaders agree to Provence. "We will call a meeting. We want it fixed too, but aren't willing to sacrifice ourselves unless *all* realms agree. It's getting dangerous for us and our families, we need assurances." I remember Lamont's words. They didn't fall on deaf ears. Maybe I am selfish, obsessive, and a bit controlling, but can't deny he's right. Our parents aren't safe, none of us are safe until an agreement is reached.

She strolls from the chair towards a painting on the wall of Blood Falls. I guess to a vampire it is beautiful or reflects what they love – blood. "When I was a girl, centuries ago, I grew up in Verboten, hiding my true self and my family. I had the ability to shift others into trolls and keep them in that form for extended periods of time. One day, our safe life was upended when two elves showed up during the great war. I saved them from the trolls and brought them home, offered them passage to Drakonia under the guise of trolls."

She turns to me and lifts her veil. The minister's ring twinkles on her finger. Its red stone shines under the light. "You've heard the story before. You know the ending."

I do. Swallowing the shock, not seeing her face, but realizing I finally understand why she is so interested in me and how she knows the depth of my connection to magic. Her hazel eyes, olive skin, and wisps of hair beneath the sides of the veil reflect the red from the painting behind her. She was a realm walker like me. One of the first. The final nail in the coffin that forced Merla's hand into creating us. A great sea fae with access to powerful magic, she bestowed on a hybrid from each realm the status of realm walker.

My true father, the realm walker of Drakonia, M'ra is my ancestor. "Why are you only telling me this now?"

"Times have changed. If the veils are weakening, we must right the wrongs done to realm walkers. Merla's spell warned the realms no harm must come to us or our children or the realms would be destroyed. That destruction is starting. They will topple," she says, her words echo in my head and I can't describe how I feel. It's pink berries and red heat mixed together.

She has no clue what I've done or doesn't let on that she does. The spell isn't specific how the realms will fall. *Am I the reason?* The brick taken from the bottom of a tower so it leans and collapses? Marilisa whines about the tree. Is that a sign it's collapsing? "Serenity Tree is shrinking at a fast pace. Are we connected to the tree?"

"Elf legend says all life is connected to the tree. If there's a grain of truth to that the tree's health is a warning. I have a meeting with the other leaders. I can bring them over if you will salvage Drakonia's veil. It will show them it is the young realm walkers we should lean on. Your parents' magic is growing weak." She takes a seat in the chair across from me.

This is working better than I planned. "I don't think I can do it alone," I reiterate, holding all the cards. "I need the others and if we do this as a measure of good will, how does that help us?"

"I will speak for you, show them what you did and plead on your behalf for Provence."

That might be convincing and I can take the opportunity to stretch and form the space between the realms at that pole. No one would be wiser. "I'll try and patch the veil in Drakonia, but I want a meeting with all the leaders if we are to mend the veils in all the realms. We won't do it unless they agree to our terms."

She nods her head. "Agreed."

I doubt as one of the first realm walkers she fully understands how much power they had...we have. Most of them to this day have no idea the power in their pinky. Lamont's energy blast to my chest is my own doing. I taught them how to transform, shield, form energy bubbles, and rip the seams of the realms open.

At the veil, I press my hands over the fissure, a rip in the seam between Drakonia and Canida, small cracks stretch across Verboten's and Thraves' borders. My handywork is beautiful. A perfect line extending along the seam. I can't make it look easy so I keep my hands pressed for many moments before the seam begins to mend. M'ra didn't come in person. She is watching from a holocall.

I put on a good show as the seam comes together and force energy between the seams, expanding the area from the inside out. There was no way for her or anyone to see this. All they'll see without realm walker vision is the mend. If they won't give us Provence, we'll make our own realm, taking parts of theirs.

I smile inside as the last of the fissure comes together and the veil in Drakonia is restored.

15

My physical body spent, and my revenge on the wolves taken captive not yet well thought out, I spend the first night in days in the inbetween. Ryel's violet soul sphere glows. It's the only light in the room. Its warmth calms me, smooths the aches in my body, and pushes me into a deep sleep.

I don't remember having a dream, but when I wake it's clear. I don't waste time molding and refining a holding cell in which to torture them. The walls resemble a cave carved from erosion. Stalactites of silver drop from the ceiling, shining under the crystals embedded in the walls. They aren't my only tool. I have a room filled with magic devices.

Hackey's lawyer sits at the table of the meeting room. His long legs stretched under the table. No suit today. He looks like any other hybrid wolf from Johnston's Pass, but he's not. He is enough lycan to pass. It's the small things, hidden well beneath the façade. I've guessed he's mixed with dragon because of his enormous size. Most lycans or dragons mixed with fae, troll, or elf are smaller in size. But his ears aren't rounded like a normal lycan, so maybe somewhere in his ancestry is a hidden fae or elf gene.

"Nice of you to join me," he says, sarcasm dripping like melted sunshine.

"Do you always hang out here?"

"I like to come here and work. Sit please." He offers with a large hand, not the calloused hands of a builder but smooth and, I imagine, soft as the skin on mine.

His hair isn't mussed but it's not styled. Curls spring at the ends. "The three lycans were taken within a two-hour gap based on witnesses. The time frame could be less. Hackey spent the evening at Nothing but Suds, a bar in eastern Canida not far from his home. This footage was pulled from his comicay."

I know Nothing but Suds. It's strictly a bar and serves mostly specialty brews. Hackey's tall, muscular frame walks into the bar as if he's uncomfortable in his own body and slides gracefully onto a stool. Hackey's not graceful, ever. His footfalls are heavy, his movements exaggerated, but the body and face are him.

"It's enough evidence for them to drop the charges," he says.

"How soon?"

"As soon as I meet with the council. Public opinion is split. Many want to crucify him, but others believe in his innocence. I'm not sure where I stand. I think maybe it was someone, someone with a stronger motive."

Me. That's what he's saying, but I was in Lols, following a vampire and trapping her in a web. I can't prove that. "You think it was me."

He lifts a thick, manicured brow. "I didn't say that. Lately you've been MIA. You don't owe me an explanation. I'm not sorry the lycans are missing. Didn't like them much anyways. Take this as a warning, advice from a confidant. You're a person of interest and it's not only the purebloods watching. The hybrids aren't sure where you stand and if you'll be there."

I think of myself as a cunning instructor and give myself the credit for Hackey's sharp observations and using the full hilt of his realm walker senses to find the tunnels. I didn't even know they existed. The underground brook, yes, but not tunnels carved from its path. The walls aren't smooth but rough, exposing varying layers and colors of rock. A glassy layer reflects the light I make. Remnants speaking the past, telling the story of what this was before the realm walkers. A treacherous place coated in danger. Perils and pitfalls at every step.

I see their forms surrounded in a high energy bubble. They emit low energy heat radiating Canidan prairie grass yellow, Navarin sunshine gold, and Blood Falls red. A fourth heat signature, small and violet-blue, moves towards me. The three lycans are tucked in a cavern without an opening. Another skill I taught the realm walkers – molding matter. If anyone thought to search down here, they'd never find them.

The tiny violet-blue figure rounds the curve and stops, her hazel eyes absorbing the colors of the tunnel.

I'm not on alert or forming a protective shield. She isn't here to harm me.

"I thought you might want help?" Jine offers.

Like she offered Hackey? Or am I wrong about him? Is she the mastermind, or did they plot together?

Hackey's moments in Nothing but Suds was her in his body. I'm mega impressed, remembering the day I taught them to transform. Jine turned into a small fuzzy lapdog with a fluffy tail. Now, she's transforming into Hackey and wearing his comicay.

"You already have. Go home. It's better you don't know what happens next."

She nods, a smile tugging at the corners of her lips as if waiting for something more.

"You've spent time practicing."

She nods. "And Hackey. You've been preoccupied and absent. We need a leader and like it or not that's you. We knew we had to help, probably shouldn't have tried to…" She doesn't finish her thought. "We have your back the way we should, now and always." An apology of sorts. I accept it, glad she's made the correct choice.

Teal dissipates and I move through the rock of the cavern.

An energy bubble surrounds them, but I don't immediately pay attention to them, something else catches my eye. In the wall to their right is a fossil's beak, large enough to eat a human. The prehistoric beast one of the many hazards met by our ancestors. Rock molds around bones, something like the bone structure of dragon wings. They are large, matching the beak and skeleton head. All life here dead, gone with the creation of realm walkers. They weren't important to the testy, powerful fae.

I turn my head to the muffled voices of the lycans. They aren't so powerful and cocky now. I convert Hackey's energy bubble into a portal and move them to my hidden prison designed especially for them.

16

I crack off a shard of silver from the stalactite and press it into the lycan's hairy, naked leg. He snarls a low, threatening growl. It rumbles, vibrating the floor beneath my feet. I don't say anything as I press the sharp edge further into his flesh. A trickle of blood dribbles and meanders to the floor. I'm not hungry for their deaths yet, only for torture.

Silver is the one thing that will kill them, painfully, but in small quantities it won't kill quickly. The poison will move through their veins, pump through their hearts and weaken them. I will continue my silver assault, languish in their pain. Silver festers, but fire burns. I will watch them partially heal, then reopen the wounds.

I open the bronze lid of the magical cylinder and drop the milky powder in and chant in old fae words. A blue flame rises, it moves through the room like a serpent. Its head splits into three distinct heads and necks. The mouths snap, hungry for their targets. When they find them, they burrow inside. Energetic flames light up their chests, fire nips at the air, and their screams excite me.

Noise like a swarm of locusts rubbing their bodies fills my ears as the shadows hiding in my soul spread their wings. Their song reaches a fever pitch then climaxes and drops off.

The blue flames lick the air around the lycans, simmer and die, leaving their chests black and flaked. Their faces in anguish, I smile. They will heal. Even with the silver cut they will heal. Mostly.

I will continue until their bodies no longer heal.

The curved blade and jagged teeth of the Scythe of Immortality shines, Ryel's violet flashes against its sharp edges. It tempts me to touch it, pick it up again. The memory of what happened last time is still fresh in my head. I don't touch it with my hands but draw it upwards with energy. The smooth jade handle at eye level. It is so simple in design, yet holds so much power.

I have the scrolls, they lay on the floor in a pile. I steal time to study them. The lawyer's and Jine's words are a warning and reminder to get my shit together.

I can give a few minutes to the scrolls. I tell myself I won't lose track of time.

A dictionary of old fae words by my side, I unroll a scroll, then another, until I have a few spread out. One is a drawing of a place called Marsay. An ancient land, but no coordinates to tell of its location. Another a drawing of the ascendant designed to take one to Tranquility and another a diagram of the fruit from Serenity Tree.

It will take a while to decode each one. My initial thoughts, these are failed attempts to create life from death.

A drawing of a pickaxe on another. Its pearl handle and wooden head are drawn by a different hand. It grabs my attention.

It rests against the wall in my room between shelves.

I think to use it more than once to pull Ryel from her soul sphere. To see her again, hear her voice again, but choose against it, not knowing what might happen to her. I'm still unsure, but I know it won't bring her back, return her to her body.

A black shadowy hand hangs over a scroll, its pointy finger revealing words penned across the bottom.

The reverser pulls the soul out of its sphere but doesn't return it to another. It doesn't reunite soul and body. After failed attempts, its designer gave up.

I think maybe that's where the wraiths come from. Souls pulled from their spheres, even good souls who spend too many years wandering the realms, can turn dark.

Eventually they learned to trap souls by taking a series of stones from each realm and placing them in specific locations around the soul. These souls went on to the Otherworld or Tranquility. The circle traps them, but doesn't force them into breathing bodies. The author of the scroll signs with the name Sulien. Is that the man from my vision?

Is the scythe the embodiment of his experimentation? Who was he? Is the mark of the Scythe of Immortality on his chest important? Are the other marks? Are they simply decoration like people in Lols? Are they the secrets to life after death? Whoever he was, he came to the middle realms from a place called Marsay. From the drawings, it is a place filled with highlands and a central valley. A dense fog separates the highest lands from the lower lands.

Pegasus, large creatures with wings, lived just beneath the fog. The people used them to travel over the valley. The drawing is of a magnificent beast similar to a horse in Lols only larger given the dimensions provided. The text warns they are testy and keen to be unhelpful if they don't trust the want-to-be rider. They use their powerful wings to create a downdraft known to knock people over when unwilling to help.

The scroll with descriptions of Marsay has a different name than the other. Printed on the bottom, not in old fae, is Leif. The print of the words slightly different than old fae, yet the same. Who are these ancient people, and what is Marsay? It describes it as the inner realm. The mysterious place I've wondered about. If there are middle realms and an outer realm, then there must be an inner. Is that code for the place where Provence now stands? Yet, from the description, it can't be, nor the pole at the other end. If I can find this Marsay place, maybe I can lead us there, away from the middle realms.

"Maybe you were something more than all of us. A life belonging to this inner realm. I know you didn't know anything of it, but that lightning bolt speaks of this realm called Marsay. In my vision the man had the same lightning bolt," I say to Ryel's bright violet soul sphere. It is all I have left of her and now maybe I have the tool to bring her back. The Scythe of Immortality and the scrolls telling how to use it.

Using what Marilisa taught me, I listen at the higher frequency for Ryel's response, but it never comes. Is it my connection to the wraith? The man said I am tainted. Does that hinder me from hearing her? It stops me from ever using the scythe. However, I'll figure out the scythe. If it takes an untainted pure soul, I'll find that soul.

17

The blue light of the sarcanthum shines in her hair. Her skin darker with the absence of sunlight. Moonlight bathes her arms and cheeks in a soft glow. We are perfect creatures, made to blend into any environment, any realm, and controllers of energy and matter. We can mold either to our will.

"I'm starting to understand your voice. At first, I hated you, but now I see it's not you, it's the hatred of the purebloods. I've done everything right, always, and I'm treated badly because of who I am. Their true colors are showing. Even the Vizier had me brought in for questioning. Me!" Pain muddles in her face and fire flashes in Marilisa's eyes. Not at me but for them. The realm leaders and purebloods.

Sadness and betrayal froths in her voice. She is as pure a soul as any can be. The reason she's always annoyed me. In the moment I feel sadness, not for me but for her, like her emotions are flowing into me. I am tainted, can never touch the scythe again, but she can. He said the purest of souls can use the magic. I don't know yet how I'm going to get her to use the scythe, but listening and empathizing are a start.

Marilisa pushes her hands into mine and holds them. "Thank you." Heat radiates through my palms from the simple gesture.

I search her face, meet her gaze and hold it. "It will only get worse. What we did today won't please them long and I fear the hairline fractures in the veil will continue." Earlier, the six young realm walkers came together to mend veils. I urged them not to work too fast, nor mend them all in a day. It's dangerous for the purebloods to know our strength and more dangerous for the realm leaders to know. If we work slow and steady we give them something they want and, in return, I hope they will meet our demands. The longer they suffer and fear the more chance we have.

Realm Walker

"I fear you're right. It's not you or us causing Serenity to shrink or the veils to crack, but their distrust and hate for us. They are causing it to happen."

She is seeing things my way. I squeeze her hands in mine. Her fingers loop in my palms. "It will get worse for us and the hybrids but we have to stick together."

She offers me a halfhearted smile before walking towards her family's trella.

The door closes behind her and I leave to take care of other business. When I first met Ryel, she offered to prove she was a hybrid of seven realms. A natural born realm walker. I insisted there was no need for that but the time had come for me to find the evidence she spoke of.

The familiar street in Johnston's Pass, Canida, sets my mood on edge. Its warm delight heats my core but Ryel's absence turns the heat into hate-filled flames. Corner streetlamps shine on the wet road. My mind returns to the day I met Ryel, my eyes find the spot we stood and talked. 'You Cyrus?' were the first words she said to me as she studied me with a curious eye, her tight jeans showing all her curves.

I step closer to Morry's Pub where her mom works. Music playing inside is a quiet hum outside. The grain in the wood slabs on the outside of the bar give it a relaxed feel. This is a place hybrids frequent, not many purebloods. I transform, hiding myself under the face and body of a lycan with pointed ears.

A tall woman with a full figure stands behind the bar, her back to me as she fills a frosty mug with Hops. The lights dim and music thumps over the conversations. A few lycans sit at the bar and two of the eight wooden tables have customers.

I slide onto a stool at the bar.

"What can I get you?" the woman asks, her breasts nearly falling out of her shirt. Close up, it is easy to see she is Ryel's mom. They have the same chin, blonde hair, and shade of skin.

"Hops."

She winks and spins around, grabs a frosty mug and fills it from the tap before sliding it across the bar to me. "Haven't seen you before," she says, more as a question. Her eyes zero in on the pointed tips of my ears before she offers me a half smile and scoots towards another customer.

In Johnston's Pass they've always been leery of outsiders, especially purebloods. Behind the bottles of liquor and taps of the various lagers is a mirror. A crack runs through the middle and webs into tiny fractures. It reminds me of the hairline fractures in the veils.

Realm Walker

The minor mending we did got us a truce of sorts that they signed. It will hold up legally in any realm as each leader signed it.

I don't have any business with Ryel's mom and leave after finishing the first frosty mug. My visit was more to see her for myself and make sure she wasn't home. To meet her, even if she didn't know she was meeting me. My business is going to Ryel's house in search of proof. Something that gives me a clue about the lightning bolt and Marsay.

I run my hand across the pillow on her bed. It doesn't look like her mom has changed a thing in her room. Her clothes hang in the closet. Pillows are fluffed against the headboard and the curtain drawn. The entire room smells like her. I could stay here indefinitely and inhale her sweet scent but eventually her mom will be home and probably attack before asking what someone is doing in her house. Lycans are predators and don't ask unnecessary questions, especially in Johnston's Pass.

I sift through the drawers, boxes in the closet, under the armoire, behind the mirror, the vent, and find nothing. I pull up her mattress, look under her pillows, and find nothing. Not that I know what I'm looking for. Sitting on the edge of her bed, my hands folded between my legs. I need to think like her. Where would she put something special?

It's my thinking that's off. She and her mom had a good relationship, no need to hide things from a person she trusts. Ryel most likely learned about her ancestors and what she is…was… from her mom. In the living room is a thick table. The top lifts, opening to a cubby. I remember it from when I stayed with her after she entered six realms in one night to help her get through the burning of the passports on her chest. Inside the table is a notebook and a pen.

I turn the first page. Curly drawings surround round bubbly writing. Ryel's family tree. I flip to the next page. It is filled with the same bubbly writing. Ryel's name is at the top. Her mom and dad below. A legend is drawn in the left-hand corner with symbols noting magics and realms. Next to each name are a series of symbols matching those in the legend.

Impressive. Mom can work metal like a magnet or bend and twist it with her mind. Dad, before becoming a vampire, wasn't as impressive but he could read minds and see future events. More interesting is that he has tattoos. She drew them in the book with a big question mark. Too bad they didn't keep him from dying.

I stuff the notebook inside my coat and portal to the cave where I keep the lycans. One lies on the floor in an awkward position, his legs pulled into his chest. The other two lean against the wall. One's chin rests on his chest. The other's head is fallen on his shoulder.

The metal box I opened earlier is closed. I set the box to open on my exit. It released a toxin with the added ingredient of silver shavings. The toxin paralyzes and the silver embeds in their lungs. They are one-step closer to death.

18

Large trees with floppy leaves stand on either side of the door and knee-high plants with yellow flowers surround the house. A woman with lavender hair streaked in silver from age answers the door.

Ryel's mom's side of the tree went back many generations. Every generation were lycans, some mixed with dragon or troll or elf, fae, even harvester, and all types of magic, but dad's side was a different story. Ryel had notes and names for her mom's side but a blank for her father which is what brings me to her grandmother's house. A woman who doesn't even know Ryel existed.

Ryel was resourceful, so I don't even ask myself how she traced her lineage. I recognize the grandmother's name, as over the past year we've made alliances with many hybrids. She is one. I pose as a hybrid doing a survey. The woman looks pure fae but Ryel's notes say she has the ability to glamor her appearance. She can also portal. It's a unique combination. Glamouring isn't something any pureblood can do.

She welcomes me with a warm smile. The woman is good, obviously a passer. "I'm so glad we're finally doing something about this. Hybrids have always been treated so bad. Would you like tea?" she asks as she shows me into an airy room, the large door open and sea breeze blowing the curtains.

A chaise and two chairs face the lavender sea. "Thank you, but I'll pass."

Directing me to one of the chairs, she sits in the other. Her frame dainty and curves small. Ryel got her voluptuous figure from her mom. I start with the questions. My eyes drawn to a painting behind her. It is an empty beach with white sands and green-ish blue waters. A sailboat in the distance. Nothing from the middle realms. It looks like a scene from Lols. I pause my questions. "That painting. Is it Lols?"

"Yes, Greece. Many memories there. So long ago, but still so fresh on my mind."

"If I'm prying, please stop me, but I'd love to hear more," I say, hoping she'll bite for nostalgia's sake.

"I guess it wouldn't harm. You being a hybrid too. I have this ability to portal and when I was young I'd go to Lols. Everywhere in Lols. It's beautiful in its own way. I have never seen cleaner sand. Not seafoam green like here, but white like starched linen." She lets out a sigh.

"Anyways," she continues, "that's where I met him. I fell in love and wanted to stay. No one there worries about magic and hybrids. They're ignorant." She chuckles. "Most are. But he was different. He had a tattoo like lightning and markings all over his body. He could spit lightning from his hands and do things I'd never seen or heard of… One day he disappeared. He went for sandwiches and never came back. Heartbroken, I returned to Navarin and nine months later had my twins."

A lightning tattoo, like Ryel. Other than the passports it was the only mark on her body. I'd explored every centimeter of it. "Twins."

Her lips curl into a gentle smile. "Yes. They are grown men now, families of their own. I don't know what kind of magic their father had, but it wasn't like anything else and powerful. He'd never tell me. Said he was born that way. Strange how I left here to leave magic and prejudices behind me and I fell in love with magic in Lols." She chuckles lightly.

Who would have thought? I knew magic existed in Lols. It isn't a secret. I was sent to London to find out if vampires were killing hybrids. Their souls shades of blue, meaning magic. It is a prison realm for hybrids who live among those without magic. Side by side. I ask her the next couple survey questions and from the corner of my eye the painting changes. The waves crest, their white tops move with the wind and the boat appears closer. A breeze sweeps over the sand, shiny white fragments lift into the air, exposing a small metal tube with filigree around the lid. "I think I'll take that tea after all."

"Of course," she responds and strolls to the kitchen.

Once she's gone, I approach the painting. The waves gently move, the tide rolls in and out. I touch my hand to the bottle. My chest catches, as if pinched like someone is twisting my heart. In front of my eyes a translucent thread forms and glides toward the painting. I freeze and can't move a single muscle as the cord stretches further into the painting until I'm in it. The sparkling sand of the beach isn't hot against my feet. The bright sun doesn't warm my head as I face the vast sea, larger in the picture. I watch the boat rock on the waves.

My entire body is translucent. I don't sense the steady thump of magic. The rhythm in sync with my own heartbeat. I know I'm powerless in the picture, just as I was in the tunnels beneath Drakonia. The prickly sensations match Drakonia. It is the same type of magic.

Glancing over my shoulder, I see myself staring at the painting. My hazel eyes glaze over. My body isn't with me. Is it a trick? The small bottle is by my foot in the sand. I pick it up. It's cool to the touch. As soon as I hold it in my hands the sky grows dark, clouds move in and blot out the sun. Wind sweeps sand through me. The painting is a gateway that's pulled my soul from my body in a form of astral projection. This isn't a pureblood trick but something of a powerful hybrid.

It isn't a fae spell and I think it must be something from the inner realm – Marsay. It's hidden somehow from everyone, including me, if it still exists.

The boat vanishes on the water and six people appear before me with chalices in their hands. Some tattooed, others not, with short, pointed tips on their ears. Fae and another life subspecies. They don't flinch when I move closer, as if they don't notice me at all. A cauldron between them; a glance inside shows a bloody heart, tip of an ear, partial wing from an ice dragon, horn of a fae unicorn and swatch of inked skin.

Words spoken in old fae pound in my ears from the sky as thunder and sparkly dust falls into the cauldron. The blood sacrifices form a bubbling green liquid. Each person dips their chalice into the cauldron, and once everyone's is filled they drink. Thunder crashes while words in old fae are spoken by the six.

The sky lights up in teal. It spreads horizontally across the horizon. I don't understand all the words, but catch the important ones; veil and seal. The veil between Lols and the middle realms has existed for many centuries. No one knows exactly how long, but today I am witnessing the sealing of that veil.

Cries sound from the other side of the veil; weeping and screams - *Betrayers!* — roars in my ears louder than the thunder. The spell is very much like the one that created realm walkers and separates all the middle realms. Chills run up my spine as the six disappear. A cloaked man takes their place.

A staff made from a metal I don't immediately recognize in his hands. It is dark, yet it twinkles like silver under the cloudy sky. The handle is carved from golden stone. He lifts his head and glowing golden-brown eyes cut through the inky air between us, meeting my gaze.

He lifts the staff and speaks: "Drink it." Then hits the staff to the ground. An explosion of white light sweeps across the sand and sea, blowing me out of the painting.

I stand in her living room, reeling from the out of body experience, my soul and body intact. Light footfalls announce Ryel's grandmother's return. The small bottle is in my hand. I stuff it in my pocket and return to the chair.

19

My old stomping grounds, CIU, hasn't changed, but to enter I have to disguise myself. As a harvester I move past the receptionist. I miss our conversations over hyndra but no one needs to know I'm here. It's safer for them.

I pull the door open. Tate doesn't even glance at me as she studies something invisible to the naked eye under a powerful lens. I slide onto an empty stool near her. She turns her head and furrows her brows, studying my features. I let my glamour down for a flash, enough for her to piece together who I am.

"Cyrus," she whispers. We haven't used the comicays for important conversation since they confiscated Hackey's.

I tuck the miniature bottle into her hands and curl my fingers around it.

She smiles and nonchalantly stuffs it into a pocket inside her lab coat. It's not the first sample I've brought her. After using the Lols vampire for bait, I brought her a sample. Her lips hardly move as she speaks under her breath. "It's vamp blood but coated in magic. Some type of spell."

A spell. Who can create such a spell? The fae? "Is there enough to read anything in the magic about the spell?"

She shakes her head.

"See what you get from the new sample."

She blinks her eyes and nods. "I'll see what I can get. Anything I should know before I get started?"

"It could be anything – even commoner. I stumbled across it and something tells me it's important."

"Gotcha. I'll contact you through messenger when I find something. I had enough of the other I'm running it through ancestry, see if I get a hit."

I lift from the stool. "Good work," I say in case someone is watching. Most likely not. CIU is the department most harvesters cringe over, but I can never be too careful.

She returns to her work as I exit and return to my inbetween.

I grab the magic device from a shelf. Its feathers are soft and beak pointed. It is said the spirit of a powerful Lols sorcerer is trapped inside. Legend says the oil of nightshade wakes it up. It will flog anyone wearing the scent. In their paralysis, I rubbed the oil into their skin.

I hold the small blue-black bird in the palm of my hand. The lycans shift, their movements slow and out of control. Their mouths open and a jumble of nonsense trickles out.

Black feathers ruffle on the bird's head and its blue wings twitch. Its beak opens, releasing a war-cry. It rises in octave until the cave is filled with the screech of the bird as it lifts from my palm and dives at the closest lycan, needling it with its beak, poking and digging at its skin. The lycan's hand won't cooperate. His body works against him.

I leave the bird to its job and portal to the trella. I haven't stayed there, but have a few items of clothing in the drawers.

Surprise smacks me in the face as I enter. Marilisa's long hair stretches over the back of the couch. She doesn't bother to turn her head as I step towards her and sit near her.

Water fills her hazel eyes. Her cheeks flush. An energy field wraps around us, not one of my making but hers. My left hand rests on the couch between us. She places her right hand over it and curls her fingers beneath.

She is sweet and vulnerable.

"I need your help. There's no one else I can ask," she says in a shaking voice.

My help? I study her with a curious eye. We have come to some sort of cease-fire since she's seeing things my way. If I help her now I can call in a favor in the future.

"Sier is getting dangerous, especially for anyone who has connections to others outside the realm. I need to get two people out of the middle realms."

"You need me to help you get them to Lols?"

She nods. "Where they can live in peace and not paranoia."

A dragon and elf couple. They are the type of couple that we are fighting the battle of Provence for. The ability to create hybrids, and for hybrids and realm walkers to live under laws that support them, not the individual realms. I agree, it could be lucrative.

We meet in Provence under an invisible shield. A female elf, her dark, plaited hair hanging over her shoulder. Her cerulean eyes filled with fear of getting caught and mistrust in me. I have no reason to betray them and every reason to help. It will bring

Marilisa further to my side and one step closer to the favor I need.

Moments later, a dragon walks through the curtain, his red hair like flames. He takes the elf's hand and his brown eyes search mine. He wants to know why I am willing to help, yet is unwilling to ask and maybe ruin his chances for freedom. To live as a hybrid couple without the scrutiny of the middle realms. Months ago, no one would have questioned my motives. I was a leader, now in our ranks they aren't sure about me. The lawyer is right.

Marilisa's eyes burn into my head as she attempts to put aside her distrust of me and give me a chance to do *something right* in her mind. She is pure and I am tainted, that's why I need her and that beautiful pure soul of hers. I can almost see it radiating its glory.

"When I open the veil you will see an old school. There's a small town not far. It has a train station, from there you can find a destination in Lols that pleases you." The dragon gives me a cock-eyed glance with furrowed brows. I know he isn't clear about what I'm telling him. "A train is like the transport in Aradia, only it moves slower," I say.

He nods understanding.

I part the sky instead of creating a portal and make a curtain between Provence and Lols. This is the location of the future school and I want a curtain to Lols. Currently the only way to travel to Lols is to portal. The curtain needs to be somewhere central, where other hybrids can use it if needed.

I use energy to push the couple towards the parted sky. Teal swirls, similar to a portal, and a pinhole grows in the middle, widening until trees and green grass are visible. Once they are safely on the other side I close it, marking it so only those with blood of more than one realm can open it, similar to the meeting room I created. The purebloods don't need the exit point.

Marilisa's hand wraps around mine as the curtain closes. "How did you…? Thank you."

Her vibrant, colorful eyes bounce with the shine of the fake, steady star. They meet mine and she lifts onto her toes and plants a kiss on my cheek. Ripples of joy stretch over me.

Her rapid heartbeat thumps in my ears and I lower my head and push her long, colorful hair over her shoulder. I brush her cheek and draw a circle around her pink lips. They are soft and supple. She doesn't push me away. Our lips brush against each other as we kiss. The growing darkness in my soul recedes and light flickers. I press her closer and run my hand over her neck, soft hair falling over my arm.

20

In the following days, life doesn't get easier. We've diligently worked to close the veils, yet the leaders are as stubborn as the largest gems embedded in Verboten dirt. A meeting is set up. I have a different agenda and leave it to the elected hybrid leaders.

My mission is to find a way to return Ryel's soul to her body. The key is the scythe and the scrolls and the tattooed species and Marilisa's perfect, pure soul. Ryel said she was born with the lightning bolt. It was more than a birth mark, but gave her matching magic.

The symbols on her grandfather and the ones on the man in my vision have magic attached.

Tate had interesting results. The wolf blood sample contained mostly lycan blood with traces of commoner and dragon. It is weak compared to lycan blood, but enough to harm vampires. The sample from the painting is more curious. It contains blood of a different subspecies, an unknown one. The tattooed people from Marsay is my assumption, as I scour Lols to find a single one. To trap it and find my answers.

I don't use a magic weapon on the lycans today. It is a day of rest. They are growing weak. The silver sketches on their skin and fragments in their lungs is keeping them from healing. Their slow, agonizing death is a joy and I'm not ready for them to die yet.

I've been tracking a vampire for the past day, hoping it might lead me to one of the tattooed. Tate's results showed their blood is spelled. It allows them to walk in daylight. There is no known spell for that. Nothing showed in ancestry about its origin. No connection to the middle realms, anyways. My assumption is the tattooed people have a spell of sorts and a treaty with commoner vampires.

The sun lowers, its red and gold hues spreading across Lols' horizon. The vampire stands at the edge of an abandoned lot as I watch from the roof across the street. In moments, a veil parts, revealing a tall mirror-glass structure. A fountain spits water into a pond and flowering bushes edge the sidewalk leading to a double door entryway.

I transform myself into a fly and buzz over the threshold before the veil vanishes and the lot returns to an empty place filled with weeds. I marvel at the complexity of the structure and respect the magic it takes to make wards strong enough to hide something so magnificent. It increased my feeling that I'm not wrong. These tattooed commoners have something to do with vampires walking in the light of day.

I focus my compound fly eyes into one single vision as the door closes. My tiny wings don't carry me fast enough to the threshold. I slip through a slim crack between the door and frame.

Outside, the mirrored building appears as a huge office space. Inside, it has modern large tile flooring and recessed lighting. A young man with long blond braids sits in a swivel chair.

In the middle realms, each realm has a capitol and its own form of government. It makes sense these commoners with magic would do the same, only they have no curtains separating their borders and can come and go. Did they get along? Lycans and vampires hate each other and hunters exist, so these factions would have to come together and cooperate, even dismissing their distaste for each other.

I lose sight of the vampire I followed in. Voices down a wide hall catch up to me. I follow them into a large meeting room with a long table. The vampire pulls a hand through her short, dirty-blonde hair. From across the table, a man with shoulder-length dark hair growls beneath his breath at her. A Lols lycan with tainted blood no doubt, by his alpha beast display. I perch on the wall mold separating cream paint from blue paint.

"He couldn't come himself," grouches the lycan to the vampire. His nose twitches in anger.

The vampire rests her brown eyes on him and narrows them, but doesn't get a word out before the dark woman at the head of the table speaks. Her hair tied in loops and braids similar to an elf, a double chin jiggling as she speaks. "We aren't here to accuse. We can't keep fighting amongst ourselves, revealing our true natures to humans. That stunt you pulled made the paper."

The lycan snarls, "My wolves are gone! They vanished at the hands of the vampires."

"What vampire do you know would stick themselves with a tainted arrow?" The vampire rolls her eyes as she leans back in the fabric chair.

"One that wanted it to look like they were innocent. She's healed now, isn't she?"

"Stop! Both of you. Hunters. We are after hunters," the dark-haired woman commands as if she has power over both.

The lycan and vampire glance to each other, then the dark-skinned woman continues. "It's the only explanation that supports both your stories."

"We've already been down this route!" The lycan growls the words. He hits a fist onto the table, shaking the sconces in the center.

I laugh inwardly as they argue over my handywork. I hadn't thought of how Lols would handle what I did when I used the Lols wolves and vampire in my ruse to distract Drakonia. Maybe it is time for more to vanish, as they claimed the others did. I know better, they didn't vanish but were sent into Drakonia, where they perished at the hands of vampires.

As polished as M'ra makes Drakonians seem, they are still predators with a distaste for wolves. M'ra's hold on the vampires of Drakonia is strong, so the possibility exists they lived at least long enough to be questioned. No answer will point to me. I disguised myself.

The lycan and vampire depart and the dark-skinned woman puts a hand to her forehead in frustration, the arm on her gown dropping to her elbow, revealing what I'm searching for. Marks, inkings, tattoos similar to passports. They are in the same language as the scrolls and the man in my vision. This place is their headquarters.

She swivels her chair around and stands, then presses the wall. It opens to a corridor. She vanishes and I buzz through the open door I came through. The fly is a good disguise but has limitations and is hard to hold. I let go and create a portal outside the walls of the building and wait, hidden behind thick, flowery bushes.

21

I don't need the vampire or the lycan. Not this time. I wait it out until a young woman jogs down the steps. Her tight jeans leave nothing to the imagination, a leather jacket wraps her chest, and short, dark hair allows me to see a marking on her neck between her hairline and jacket collar.

Outside the wards, I follow but keep my distance. She glances over her shoulder once then crosses the street to the left. I go straight then duck inside a candle shop. My realm walker senses track her moves.

"Can I help you?" asks a female voice belonging to a plump woman with round, blue-framed glasses.

I pick up the candle I'm petting mindlessly. "Yes, I'm looking for something for my girlfriend. She loves scented flowers."

"Any particular scent? We have jasmine and lavender, narcissus?" she says, leading me to another table.

I set the candle down and pick up a white one with a strong yet sweet scent. "This one."

"Honeysuckle, always a good choice."

The woman I'm tracking stops a few blocks away. I use power of suggestion and the woman bags the candle for me. Outside the store, I drop it in my inbetween world – I'll give it to Marilisa – and return to the woman, keeping several yards from her.

The bench she sits on overlooks a small lake. She tosses crumbs at the birds who peck them from the ground. I move closer, careful not to make a sound, and envelop her with my energy. I force it into her chest like a fist. She coughs and retaliates with a blast of her own energy, not quite equal to mine.

I wear my hunter disguise and pin her to the bench. She twists her head as small branches snap under my feet when I walk around the bench to face her. "Tell me about your markings?"

She wrinkles her nose in frustration and pushes energy against my hold on her. "There's nothing to tell. I like tattoos."

Her snarkiness won't get her anywhere with me and her power isn't strong enough to break my hold on her. "You're powerful."

"So are you," she says, giving up her attempt to break free.

"I'm not your enemy, but I can be if you don't cooperate."

"If you kill me, you learn nothing. Show yourself," she orders as if she controls the situation. I don't like her spunk.

I sit on the bench beside her. "What is Marsay?"

She scoffs, "What? I've never heard of it."

"You wouldn't respond so quickly if you hadn't."

She folds her hands over her chest in defiance. I snap my fingers, taking us through a portal to the upstairs of the old, abandoned school I found.

"What the hell are you?!" she screams. It bounces off the walls of the empty room.

"A hunter and a hybrid."

"You hunt hybrids." Spittle flies into the air of the energy bubble engulfing her.

I walk in front of her, turn my body sideways, and point at the door. "On the other side are the middle realms. You tell me what Marsay is and I'll let you walk through those doors." It's a long shot but diplomacy has its ways, except with the realm leaders. The scrolls I found match the markings on her people's skin better than old fae. If her people are in Lols, what happened? Why and what the hell is Marsay?

She rubs a thoughtful hand under her chin, then behind her ear. "How do I know you're telling the truth? This place is old and dusty. Why would I think that decrepit door would lead to anything but the rest of the house?"

"Look outside the windows."

Her gaze shifts and brows lower. "All you want is to know about Marsay and I get to walk into a hidden world?"

I meet her gaze and nod. Undecided if she'll ever return to Lols.

She shrugs and opens her mouth to speak, then shuts it as a bright light envelopes us for a moment.

Another young woman steps out of the light, markings cover her collarbone and neck. She pushes her hands towards me and a strong wind drives me backwards.

Anger slithers from my core to my extremities. I've had enough pushes into walls. I gather the energy of the wind in my hands and push it at her. She stumbles backwards a few steps. Electricity blankets her hand. It crackles and sparks as she thrusts it at me in a whip.

It wraps my middle. The chorus of locusts rises in the room. I can't tell if she hears it but it's deafening in my ears. My body twitches with daggers of rage. She extends her other hand to the woman trapped in my energy and breaks my barrier.

Impossible! I absorb the energy of the room. It fills me. I am energy and matter. No elemental force can hold me. Anger writhes in me, the chorus heightens to a new pitch. My fingertips glow, their warmth fuels the blue hot flames building inside me and explode. A wave of energetic flames flashes over the room.

A stream of water meets the flames as they move to the women. Dark edges coat my vision as her eyes widen and her mouth drops open. My body heats to a fever. *No one is stronger than you.* A voice pushes through my thoughts. Hate rising to my core. I push against the door and it flings open, revealing the empty stairwell.

No one is stronger than you. The voice speaks again, taunting, louder. It feeds the heated energy pulsating from my body. I thrust the woman towards the door and shadows swarm the floor and an inky shapeless blackness meets her on the other side of the door, her screams swallowed as

she vanishes into a void. The door slams
behind her.

22

My return to the middle realms is met with chaos as the realm leaders have turned on each other. The meeting didn't go as planned. Marilisa waits in the meeting room. She rushes at me, her voice frenzied. "Where have you been? The meeting was a disaster, the leaders can't agree on anything except you and how much they hate you. The others are locked away and I'm not safe, none of us are safe. I think they've taken their comicays too. When I try and contact any of them I get nothing."

"Slow down. Who have they taken?"

"Realm walkers," she says.

"They're fine. They are realm walkers. As you hid here, they can escape the walls holding them."

"They've taken hybrids too. This is so out of hand." A tear threatens to drop from her right eye as she plops onto one of the chairs.

I drop on one knee and take her hands in mine. They're shaking. She needs my comfort. "We can collect the hybrids too. There is more power in our pinky fingers than any pureblood possesses."

I think of the woman I held captive in the fourth floor of the school. She claimed to be a warlock and Marsay the inner realm. A place her kind was locked out of centuries ago. The vision I saw at Ryel's grandmother's makes sense. The blood makes sense. It was the fae who trapped them in Lols using powerful magic.

I think of the warlocks. They too can be strong, as strong as me. The display I saw showed they have strength in elemental magic. That's why the fae locked them out. Our fate won't be like theirs. "We can take Provence as our own. We don't *need* their permission. That was a nicety."

Her eyes shine golden under the light. "No." She shakes her head. "No, if we take Provence we'll be as bad as them and we aren't. I know I didn't play along from the beginning but now I see it." Sniffles wrack her words as tears drop from her eyes. "You were right. My realm has turned on me."

She says it with such conviction it would have pulled my heartstrings had I any left. I have one agenda now. To bring Ryel back from the dead. And I'll do whatever it takes for that to happen. I stand, her warm, shaking hands still in mine. "I want to show you something."

I form a door in the wall of the meeting room and push it open. She gasps. "I created all this. Together, we can do so much more. All of us combined can create a realm of our own. We can escape and leave all the realms behind. We don't need them."

Her sniffles dry up as we walk through a field of wildflowers. I change their colors from blue to pink. "You did all this?"

Without giving her a response, I create a stream in the field of wildflowers.

She gasps and leans down, placing her fingers into the slow moving water. "This is beautiful. All that is inside you is beautiful. I understand why…" She doesn't finish her words, her expression darkening. "I can't. We can't. Life will cease to exist. All this and life will die when Serenity…"

Before the words leave her mouth, I know what she is going to say. The tree – Serenity – with her it is always Serenity. I can't say 'forget Serenity', that will set her off and I need her on my side. I don't know exactly how to bring Ryel back, but I know enough to know I need a pure soul and it doesn't get much purer than Marilisa's.

My power has grown since Ryel's death and the tree doesn't matter. Life will exist without it. Anything she thinks she knows is elf legend. "How, then, do we save the tree and get the realms to agree with us?"

"I don't know."

I fold her into my arms and create a gentle breeze that sweeps over us. "We'll figure it out. You were smart to come here. Stay here while we make a plan."

Her arms around my back and, with her head tucked into my chest, she nods.

I show her how to create and build. I don't need her connecting with the full breadth of her power but enough she will stay busy. I need to buy time, which means I need more than myself to entertain her.

23

I don't leave her side all night, and the next day I make a proposition. She agrees and we leave the hidden world, escaping into the middle realms under the guises of purebloods. Her transformation skill set not as developed as mine, I lend magic to help her stay in form.

Not a soul takes a second glance at us as we move through Provence as dragons. Lamont was always true, even though we haven't spoken since our fight. He is the first we're going to jail break.

I have connections. The ice dragon, Kierra, has always been an ally and I trust her.

Pausing at her stand in Provence, I send a cool breeze over her. She shifts her gaze from the customer and meets mine. A smile tugs at the corners of her lips.

Once the customer is gone and she is alone she greets me. "What can I help you with?"

I can't come right out and say it, as predator ears might be listening, so I say, "I'm looking for a special piece. A rare device…" I hope she gets the meaning. She has to know Lamont has been taken.

She scribbles something on paper as I speak. "We don't have anything like that here." She pushes the paper to the side and Marilisa slips it into her pocket.

Reaching for Marilisa's hand, I clutch it as we stroll to Sier as if we aren't in a hurry. Snow-capped peaks and frigid air encircle us as we walk through the curtain. I pull her toward the cave. It is an especially blustery day. A mix of snow and freezing rain pellets shower us.

Her entire body quivers from the cold. I wrap a warm energy blanket around us. Inside the cave, she pulls the paper out of her pocket. "It's worse than freezing. Is it always like this?" she asks, opening the slip of paper.

"No, sometimes it's colder and other times not as cold," I say while reading the paper. "Drop it."

"What?" she asks in confusion.

"We can't leave a trail."

She lets go. It twirls as it falls, then explodes in flames. They lick its edges and devour it.

"I'm not going to ask," she says. Her mood is better, her hands don't shake, and I think doing something focuses her mind, makes her feel useful.

We spend the day as dragons. Traveling through their maze of caves. Like harvesters, dragons live in the caves. Unlike Thraves, most of the land is too cold for running water outside the caves. Brooks and streams flow through the highlands. Crystals sparkle in the walls and streaks of metal are embedded in the smooth rock.

The cave is a labyrinth, burrowing into the belly of the highlands. According to the map Kierra drew, they are holding the hybrid leaders and Lamont in a cavern deep inside, as if he couldn't create a portal to escape.

We follow the labyrinth of caves deeper and deeper. Dragons become fewer. We stay on course, pausing to talk when passing other dragons. We haven't turned a single head and now we are in heavy enemy territory.

"Stay here," I suggest, moving my hands along the rock face to feel the energy and help me see beyond it.

"No. We're in this together and together we are stronger."

Why is she right? That pure soul thing. "What do you see on the other side of the wall?"

She closes her eyes, absorbing the energy. "Guards, a hallway, more guards, a walkway leading down, and more guards posted outside a cave. Its walls are thick, but I feel the energy behind them."

She is more skilled than I've given her credit for. I was and wasn't surprised when Hackey and Jine pulled off the kidnapping of the three lycans, but I taught them, worked with them. Marilisa never joined us.

"I'm going to knock out the first set of guards. You wait a few minutes and follow me through the rock, don't portal. We want the element of surprise. Once we've taken them down we can reform our clothing to match a guard's uniform and use that disguise to walk past the other guards," I say.

She peers at me with her quizzical half-moon-shaped eyes. "We need a reason to be heading to them."

She is right again.

"Food. We dress like kitchen help."

"And you know how kitchen help dresses?"

She huffs, "You aren't the only one with surprises."

Impressed, I agree.

Molding into the wall, I push through until I see the guards. Forcing energy outward,

I whack their heads together, knocking them out cold. I can't stop the smirk forming on my face.

"Impressive," Marilisa whispers as she steps out of the rock. Reforming her clothes, I follow her lead. She creates two rolling carts and loads them with covered dishes.

The next set of guards stops us, asking for orders. "The supreme dragon sent us himself, let us through." Power of suggestion is a cool trick and works on dragons too. They nod and move out of the way. They won't even remember us.

We reach the bottom of the sloped walkway, and the last set of guards takes one look at our cart and trays and opens the cave doors for us. "Leave it right inside," a bulky dragon guard orders, his red hair flaming like fire.

I smile, push past him, then force energy outward to knock their heads together, but Marilisa beats me to it. She winks at me. Immediately we drop the guises.

Lamont's lips tug into a smile when he realizes it's us. "We're here to get you out."

24

We portal them to my inbetween. With Marilisa's help, it's grown. I don't know how many it will fit, but they need a safe place and Marilisa is trusting me. If I keep showing her good deeds I'll melt away all her defenses.

"We have to get the others, everyone we can. Once the dragons realize we're gone, the word will get out and who knows what they'll do to the others," Marilisa states, her voice shaking yet ready for the next adventure.

"She's right. What can we do to help?" a dragon hybrid asks.

REALM WALKER

"Stay here. As we send others, welcome them. Put your minds together and think of solutions," Lamont replies, then turns to me with a narrowed, untrusting eye. No doubt he blames me for all that happened since I bailed on them. "We can do this faster if we split up. We portal everyone here."

I like how he takes command. In the past, everyone looked to me. I was the instigator, but now it is beyond my control and not my concern. However, I need to play politics until I get what I need – my pure soul. Marilisa.

It takes longer to rescue Lamont than it did to collect everyone else, proving the realm walkers have learned from me. I've taught them to transform, taught Lamont how to open the veil to the inbetween, and Marilisa has her own tricks. She surprises me the most. With each realm walker we rescue we have one more to rescue another.

In the end, all the hybrid leaders and all six youthful realm walkers fill the meeting room. Now that everyone is safe I'm met with angry glares and hefty words. "What happened?" I ask as the hybrid leaders and realm walkers take their places at the table. I know they blame me. I wasn't there. I heard the lawyer's warning echoed in Jine.

A Canidan hybrid spits, anger flaring, "What happened to you? It was you who set it up and you who suggested we meet in person.

That Provence was a safe space. It was you who abandoned us."

He is right. My double life pulls me from the movement I started when Ryel was killed. A wraith captured my soul, the Scythe of Immortality knocked me on my ass, and then there's the warlocks. My plans and priorities have changed, but they can't know that. "I'll take that hit. I went to check out Lols."

Marilisa butts in, "It doesn't matter. We can't fight amongst ourselves or we become like them. I'm sure whatever Cyrus was doing in Lols was for all of us. Isn't that where he got the idea?"

The lycan steps back and forces his anger down. It swallows as hard as a jumbo-sized pill. I've played her well. Marilisa is defending me now.

"I'm sorry. It's late. Why don't we sleep on it and try and find a solution tomorrow?" I suggest, hemorrhaging sorrow into my tone. It is just enough empathy that tempers simmer.

I step outside into the menagerie of wildflowers and turn off the sun, creating darkness, and slip into the room where I hold the warlock. She barely lifts her eyes and doesn't meet mine, as if fearing what she might see.

I have no more use for her and see no reason to keep her around. "Look into my eyes," I say.

She turns her head, her gaze shifts, barely meeting mine. Her mouth opens. Sound takes a second before words spill.

I inhale their sweetness, fresh as fruit, tasty as salt. They are a bargain that saves her life. Valuable.

I say, "You don't remember who or what you are. You don't remember me. You only remember your name," and create a portal. The teal matter moves and grates and I push her into it. I spin it like a top and let it vomit her out wherever it stops.

25

The morning is met with arguing and heavy debate over our next step. Some on the side of taking Provence for ourselves and forcing their hands, others willing to sacrifice themselves to Lols.

"No," Marilisa takes a stand. "If you go to Lols, most of you won't have a way to return. You have magic but don't portal, there's no curtain."

She lies. She saw me create the curtain. Now is my chance to gain a good believable cover story. "She's right and Lols isn't completely safe. There are hunters and, any inkling of magic, they will kill you and ask questions later. That's why I went to Lols."

"All other hybrids are at risk and your parents along with your siblings," the hybrid leader of Aradia points out.

Our parents played by realm rules but how long before they take them into custody? She is right.

"They can go to Drakonia," another hybrid suggests.

"Who wants to live in a place flowing with commoner blood?" Jine asks. It's a solid question.

"We can set up another meeting through a holocall and smooth things over," the hybrid leader from Navarin suggests.

All chatter stops and eyes drop on her. "Like the queen of Navarin isn't one of the biggest tyrants."

A smile creases the fae hybrid's lips and she exchanges glances with Shiane. "She's pregnant. I think she'll hear us out. That's a huge bomb and one that can be manipulated."

Whispers spread over the room. "A holocall meeting it is. If we can get her to meet with us, the others will too."

The meeting set. I step outside. The patter of light footfalls follow me. I don't need to glance over my shoulder to know

Marilisa is behind me. I need her to follow me, somewhere private where others can't overhear us.

"This place is really beautiful. I'll miss it, but I hope the meeting works. We need to find peace."

"You didn't mention the curtain in Provence to Lols."

"No, we need them to think carefully before making rash decisions. If they knew there's a curtain we probably would have been trampled by all of them rushing to it."

She isn't wrong. "What I said about Lols is true. It's safe only if they don't know you have magic. What commoners don't understand they fear. They don't know of these realms and can't know, possibly ever, but we also have to accept that this may never work, leaving us with two options; taking Provence or escaping to Lols."

She cocks a curious eye at me.

"I think we need another plan. One that will take time to grow. One that has to be nurtured."

Her mouth drops at my words. "You're suggesting… Umm…" The wheels in her mind spin as she swallows my suggestion. "You do mean we…I mean I'm attracted to you but…"

I chuckle as she trips over her words. "I'm attracted to you. You're beautiful, you're perfect, and I can't think of anyone I'd rather procreate a new realm walker with. I know the circumstances are bad and we can give it time. We don't have to do this right away. Let's at least get through the meeting with the realm leaders. I promise I'll be present. I won't leave you again." I grasp her hands in mine.

She nods. I see in her face she isn't convinced, but is thinking about it.

I know it's rash and unexpected and I'm not convinced either, but a child could be my answer. A back up pure soul.

26

The warlock's last words before I portalled her were the answer I want. They confirm the thoughts consuming me. According to the warlock, a pure soul is necessary to wield the Scythe of Immortality. It was a warlock necromancer that created life from death, a man of purest soul. Sulien was his name. The mark of the scythe formed on his chest with a vision that showed him how to create life from death. It showed him how to fashion the Scythe of Immortality and imbue it with magic that would take death and recreate it into beings that could survive in a dead land flowing with blood.

For someone without the scythe mark to wield it, the soul had to be not only pure, but of strong magic. I would have the strongest of pure souls at my disposal. My own offspring, created to bring Ryel back from death in case something happens to Marilisa.

I use M'ra to persuade the chief of Thraves, as I know he'll not give me a moment of time. It seems the Queen of Navarin also has pull among the realms, more than I realized, and pregnancy has softened her, or maybe it is the celebration and high spirits of the realm as they are to welcome in less than nine months' time a diama or princess to the realm.

In Navarin, a female rules before a male. A male only takes the throne in modern ages if there is no diama. In fact, the queen's pregnancy is kept quiet until she's nine weeks along and the gender ceremony performed to announce the diama's coming to the realm with a name already chosen – Halsey.

The meeting starts with greetings, and congratulations are provided to the queen as I am sure gifts will be sent for the welcome event. Once the formalities are over the attention focuses on us.

The elected hybrid leaders join me. I feel more than see how they aren't sure if they can trust me. They want to, but my recent absences force them to reconsider my intentions.

I stare into the eyes of the realm leaders and observe their postures: shifting uneasily, rubbing fingers over thumbs, tugs on beards. I see the sharp lines and wrinkles of fear. It pleases me, strengthens me. It isn't what we planned, but I need to wrangle their emotions, strangle them with terror. "Your prisons can't hold us. You fear what you can't control. We have worked for you, solved your problems for centuries. We came to you over a year ago with a solid plan. You refused. You've fought us every step of the way and tricked us. We gave you our trust, even though you didn't deserve it, and you turned on us. Even then, we went peacefully into captivity. In the dankest, darkest corners of your realms."

I study the Navarin queen. "Do you want to bring a new diama into the hate-filled world you've created?" Shifting my gaze to the chief of Thraves, I dig in. "It is you who sent me to Lols because you distrusted the vampires. You thought they were killing others in Lols and still haven't admitted to any of the others that hybrids are being murdered. You harvest their blue soul spheres in silence."

This isn't news to M'ra, but I am sure under her veil she casts him a nasty glance.

I turn my eyes to the Supreme dragon. "You took our comicays and you've learned we tweaked them to block all of you out. However, we don't need them. Keep them. We have other ways of communicating," I say. I don't have proof they found the chip, but I'm sure they have. They've had weeks to dissect them.

The Supreme dragon narrows his eyes and shifts in his seat as the others glance disdainfully on him, as if they weren't a part of it and took the comicays of those they imprisoned.
"Fact is, you have no idea how far-reaching our magics are."

The lycan leader interrupts my soliloquy. "You win," he announces, as if he has any say in other realms or even his own. He is merely a representative. "You want Provence, take it!"

A disruption among the other leaders sparks. "I think we need a moment," the Navarin queen announces.

Hackey pauses the holocall and we wait for several moments that have everyone on edge. Fingers tap the table, legs shift, and eyes study the room. The comicay lights up and we return to the call. The queen speaks. "We will agree to allowing you one representative from each of our realms to work out a plan that is agreeable to all of us."

The harvester hybrid speaks, his words deep and resonating, "You have given us no guarantee that we can return without imprisonment to our own realms."

"Yes, we have. You can go home," the chief announces, eyeing me. I haven't been there in months.

After the meeting everyone trickles out slowly, some unsure if it is safe. I don't force any. I want them confident in their choices.

A dragon is the last to leave. He is an especially tall dragon who, in physical appearance, doesn't look to be a hybrid. His chest and back thick enough to hold a hefty set of wings. He and Marilisa speak quietly at the table.

I drop into the chair beside him. It is Marilisa who speaks. "I've made a decision."

I give her an awkward glance. *Has she told the dragon?* My proposition was private.

He swivels in the chair and faces me, his expression serious as a stone statue. "I overheard your conversation. I apologize, as I didn't mean to eavesdrop, but I want to volunteer myself as a surrogate father to leave here and join my best friend in Lols. The couple you helped escape a few weeks ago…" He pauses, inhaling a deep breath, his oversized chest filling like a balloon before it deflates to its normal large.

"I watched the realm leaders today. They won't keep their promises. We need a plan of contingency. A realm walker child hidden from them will ensure that even under the darkest of circumstances magic and life will continue."

I don't doubt his words. The realm leaders can't be trusted.

"Theios, you don't have to give up your life. You aren't a hybrid. They'll never come after you. You're completely safe." *A pureblood supporting us?* It is almost unheard of but agrees with my observations.

He drinks Marilisa in with his eyes. "I have loved you since we first met when all the craziness started. I would do anything for you and the child you will soon be carrying."

Wait? What? Is she his girlfriend, or is he an admirer? That complication makes my guts twist. With his permission, he wants me to have sex with the woman he loves for the sole purpose of creating a child. It's a buzz kill. Those were Ryel's words the first time we gave in to our burning passion for each other. I know my fate and that of the first person I have sex with, and I couldn't do that to her.

"We'll go together, you and I. We won't use magic and the child won't know what it is until, and if, the time is right."

I leave the room for the love birds to have a moment together. I will be a sperm donor for their child and hopefully they'll

have more and won't mind giving up the one.
Not that it matters.

Mechanical sex is never something I
wanted. Ryel is what I wanted; buried between
her thighs and voluptuous ass. My memories
so clear I can almost feel the nights we spent
together, exploring each other. She should
have been my first.

Marilisa agrees. She is beautiful, her
skin flawless as I caress it. She doesn't arouse
and excite me the way Ryel did, but I'd have
to be blind, without senses, to not enjoy her.
Nothing about our encounter is mechanical.
Her delicate curves coax my fingers, enticing
my lips against her skin. Her elfy scent sweet
and earthy.

She responds with moans. Her fingers
leaving a trail of heat over my skin. I indulge
in her soft, sweet-smelling skin and purring
energy. Her lips kissable. I feel everything, life,
energy, matter. It's all with me…us. The
attraction between us turned the experience
into a pleasurable one and I lose myself inside
her.

Her fingers sliding over the muscles of
my back leaving a trail of intense pleasure.
They press harder as our movements build.
Her breath hot on my neck. Our hearts beat
as one, syncing with the heartbeat of the
realms and groans escape my mouth. This is
more than sex. It's more than I ever thought.

Realm Walker

Our bodies move together, magic threads and weaves itself through us; intense and soft, pulsing and throbbing. Our passions consume us, connect us. They reach a climax so intense the edges are red and sharp and smooth as glass and soft and wet as snow. Energy ripples through the veils and curtains as the new realm walker is conceived.

27

A pencil pusher is sent to us from each realm. Someone who will do as asked by their leader. Someone without backbone.

On the bright side, construction of Provence Hall started, the ground breaking anyways, and the designs for the city are in the hands of the realm leaders to agree on or add/remove what is or isn't helpful for their people.

A bond forms between Marilisa and I. It's a thread that connects us. I feel what she feels. I wonder if my mom and Preston experienced the same thing when she became pregnant with me. I lower myself to the grass beside Marilisa, Serenity shading our heads. "How is the baby?"

Marilisa's lips curl into a smile. "Better. It's growing and not shrinking. I think she'll be OK. We did the right thing." She smiles at her belly as she pulls a hand over the tiny baby bump.

We don't speak of the baby out loud, but in gentle, targeted whispers as someone may overhear us. In Aradia it would be the plants. They listen in, and even though they keep private conversations private, they know things.

The baby must be kept secret. No one other than the three of us: myself, Marilisa and Theios can know. If all works out, I'll be like my father – "childless" – and Marilisa and Theios will be parents. Two pure souls to raise and nurture *my* pure soul.

If all doesn't work out, they'll still be parents but in Lols, away from the middle realms where the child will grow up unaware of its heritage until the time is right.

Marilisa rests a head on my shoulder, her long hair spilling to the ground. *I can't feel her moving but her magic flows through me. Colors are brighter, sounds clearer, and energy moves — and smells. The most delightful, sweet aromas. More powerful than the candle.* She throws in the last bit since I gave her the candle from Lols as a gift. She doesn't know the story behind it.

Her words catch me off guard, as she's never spoken into my head. My mind wanders again to my mom and Preston. Is this a realm walker to realm walker thing or does it happen to realm walkers who make a baby with a hybrid or pureblood? *Her?*

I think so. I think Terra is a good name. It means goddess of the earth in commoner.

It has a nice ring to it… What if it's a boy?

We'll call him Terra too. She laughs. Its sweetness rings like chimes. *Maybe we'll call him Terry. That means leader of the tribe in commoner. This baby will be a leader, someone with magic from all realms who will finish our work.*

Pregnancy brain makes her more wistful than ever. She, or he, will be the same age as the next diama of Navarin. Will they work together? Will they be friends, enemies, or indifferent? *I like Terra. Terra O'Malley has a nice ring.*

It does. I agree.

Life is almost too good. The realm leaders have left everyone alone. Construction is finally started and I have the scrolls interpreted.

I nearly forgot about the lycans and, after four days, found them clinging to a thread of life. At that point it was almost a mercy killing when I knocked off another silver stalactite, driving through each of their hearts.

Their last breaths peaceful and I didn't need the thrill of their submission and suffering. Black shadows rising off their bodies and swimming across the cave floor.

I portalled their dead bodies to Lols, throwing them into the mouth of Mt. St. Helens.

A Canidan Hops in my hand, I chug it, legs hanging over the edge of the cliff as I've done with Metford so many times. We haven't met in months.

"Didn't expect to see you here," says his familiar voice. It gives me a sense of peace, or maybe that is my connection to Marilisa and the baby.

I hand him a Hops. "How is the instructor job going?" I ask.

"Not as exciting as your life, but I'm teaching young harvesters to save souls and it has its own reward."

He puts the drink between his legs and I note his comicay. The design slightly different. The dragons returned our comicays, the upgrade intact, but we don't use them for private business. "How's construction?" he asks.

"It's starting. Is that a new comicay?"

"Yeah. They're collecting the old ones and giving us these. New technology, I guess."

He isn't the most motivated of harvesters, so I doubt he cared much about a device he doesn't understand, made in Sier. "Can I see it?" I ask.

He shrugs and slides the device from his wrist. It doesn't contain our upgrade. I return it. "What are they doing with the old ones?"

"Recycling them, I guess. Fashioning them into something else."

The part of me that waits for the shoe to drop angers. They were collecting them to seek out those helping us. To find the hybrids.

28

The Supreme Dragon nearly jumps out of his chair as my portal vanishes, leaving me in his office. "Your plan is shit! What are you doing with the comicays?"

He stands, revealing his full height. He is at least forty cm taller than me, and far bulkier. It doesn't intimidate me, as I stand my ground. I hope my child has my fight and her mother's spirit. She'll need it.

"I don't make the decisions in my realm. I execute the decisions made," he barks with a flame.

"By voting citizens which excludes all hybrids and realm walkers," I bite back.

The commotion brings thick dragon soldiers into the room. "Don't touch me," I snarl through gritted teeth and vanish through a portal.

I call the pencil pushers, realm walkers, and hybrid leaders together. "They're replacing comicays."

The pencil pusher from Sier raises his hand. He's a sorry excuse of a dragon and probably a hybrid. Tall, but thin. "The old ones are outdated."

The dragon hybrid leader glowers at him with an are-you-that-stupid glare. "No, they aren't. They are searching for those who helped us."

Lamont pipes in, his tiny eyes staring down at the pencil pushers. "Let the realm leaders know we won't put up with arrests, questioning, or anything else related to the comicays. Go!"

The dragon jumps out of his chair, followed by the others.

"When we were arrested the word got out to pull the chip. They shouldn't find anything, or not much. If everyone was smart and not lazy, it's not a problem, them collecting comicays. Let them," he says, expressing my own thoughts.

"The arrests scared a lot of us around the realms. Word spread quickly and chips were pulled immediately," Jine offers. The warning not to use them for private business was given when Hackey was taken. His was the first.

"Any word of arrests or the like, I want to know immediately," I say, sure the realm leaders will make a mistake, mess up in some way.

I walk the length of the circular foundation of Provence Hall. It stands exactly where we placed it on our original plans, in the center of Provence.

Stunts like they were pulling with the comicays are why I'll never trust them. I sit on the framed steps of Provence Hall as the fake spell bound sun lowers.

Footfalls approach, throwing me from my thoughts. "I have to hand it to you. It seems you did it."

It is a long way from being finished. Hybrids and realm walkers still have no rights. My mind for the past few hours has argued with itself over taking the area, blocking the curtains so purebloods can't pass. "Are you feeling *fatherly* tonight?" I ask Preston as he parks himself next to me. He and M'ra both warned me, practically pleaded with me, not to pursue equality and Provence.

"No, I stroll through here sometimes at night and imagine what it will look like when it's finished. I was doubtful of your vision. Not anymore."

I change the conversation, thinking of my child. "When Mom was pregnant, did you know? Was there a connection?"

"Because we're both realm walkers? I think that connection exists between all parents. It might be stronger when stronger magic is involved."

"Do you still feel it with me?"

"Not in the same way. Sometimes I see images or feel a tug like a loose thread. It's a bond. One day, when you have children, you'll understand."

Isn't that a fatherly response? One day I'll understand. Don't they always say that? No, my connection is different, stronger. I am convinced the fetus growing in Marilisa's womb is speaking to me. "Don't stay up too late," I josh and leave.

Ryel's sphere shines bright from the shelf. It's never dulled, not even a teeny pinch. Nor has it spoken. If there is a way to communicate with unharvested souls, I can't do it. I've tried. "One day I'll bring you back," I say to her. I don't know if she hears me.

When I wake up in the morning, the sphere has moved. I'm sure. It sits on a base on my shelf and it's not on the base but beside it. I never touched it. I am tainted and, like the scythe, don't want to poison her soul sphere. The tiny cylinder of blood I took out of the picture drops on its side. The lid on tight, nothing spills. I place it on a higher shelf. "Are you trying to talk to me?"

The sphere doesn't move, doesn't shine brighter, or do anything different. I've been reading up on the magic of soul spheres, searching for anything that can help me, and coming up blank.

I pick up the tiny cylinder of blood and hold it between my thumb and pointer finger. I pull the lid off. The vision told me to drink it. I put a single drop on my finger and bring it to my tongue. Its bitter taste numbs my tongue. I'm no longer in my room. My mind and soul in a waterfall-filled colorful world. In my hand is a jeweled cross-shaped object. Its weighty in my grasp. Words imprinted on it read: *Inside is hidden, unlock and find.* The vision evaporates and I'm returned to my room, staring at Ryel's sphere, her violet light flashing in my eyes. Unsure what it is I drink another drop. A different vision appears, this one I see what I'm sure is the future. The same disembodied voice says: *The darkness and light must come together, only one can prevail.*

Shivers run over my spine. Great magic means sacrifice, both I and my daughter will have to make those sacrifices. She will have to be strong enough to do what needs to be done.

Speaking loud into the air, I summon the wraith, "You never told me what I wanted to know or why you chose me."

I am met with silence, then whispers fill the room from every corner. *You already know the answer.* "What is it you want?"

Laughter fills my ears and bounces off the walls. *The time isn't right. Be patient.* The voice sounds in concert with other voices, almost like echoes, but I only let in one wraith. Dread slow walks my legs and rests in my chest.

29

I tug the silver collar from under the black jacket with silver filigree on the arm, fan it out, and transform my pants into matching fae regalia. This time the pants aren't as tight as what the queen made us wear the time she invited us to Navarin.

My hair tucked into a low ponytail, the color changes to chestnut, and the tips of my ears mold and form small points. I thought of going as myself but changed my mind. It will bring too much attention. As a fae, I blend in with the crowd. People won't be guarded around me.

My door ajar, small footsteps patter the hallway. A very pregnant Marilisa walks past my room. More often than not she stays with me. No one is to know she's pregnant and so, to be herself, she doesn't leave my inbetween world often. "What are you all dressed up for?" she asks, a hand soothing her rounded belly.

"The new diama's inauguration ceremony. It's one of the largest, most festive celebrations in Navarin." I grab her hands and twirl her under my arm then catch her. "You should come too. As a fae you can be pregnant in public." I place a hand on her belly. "You are carrying the new realm walker and savior of life."

She rolls her eyes. "Go ahead," she says, taking a step back.

As my date she has to match. I fit her with a silver gown adorned in the same filigree pattern only in black. She finishes the rest, transforming herself into a fae beauty. Her delicate features natural with the small tips on her ears.

Music, spirits, and food flow through all of Navarin. The lavender seas sparkle brighter and fairy dust is thick in the air. Fae dance on the grounds surrounding the white palace. Marilisa's hands in mine, we twirl under the darkening golden sky, replaced with bright stars that seem to twinkle to the rhythm of the music, or maybe that is me.

Realm Walker

My spirit is high. Marilisa's presence has that effect on me. I smile, laugh, joke, and feel as though a cloud is under my feet.

There won't be such a celebration for our own child born in secret, but she will be more important than the diama. Shelled horns blare and fae rush to the balcony. The queen, dolled up in a rose gold dress and wearing a crown of diamonds, walks onto the balcony, the tiny child in her arms.

The queen is breathtaking if you can get over her bitch. Folded in her arms is a shimmering pink blanket. The king, a hand behind the queen's back, strolls onto the balcony with her. He lowers the blanket and takes the baby in his arms. Holding her up, he announces: "Welcome your new diama!"

Comicays pan the infant, her tiny face and bald head on screens around the courtyard. Her tiny little pink nose scrunches and miniature hands brush against her cheeks as if the uncoordinated tiny fae is looking for a finger to suck. For a baby, maybe she's cute. I haven't spent any time around them. The queen and king retreat, then reappear without the child. I assume she is with her nannies and wet-nurse.

Through the thread connecting us, I send a message to my child: *Keep the diama in her place always.*

A sharp metaphorical dark radiates through my core. I double over in pain.

Marilisa's eyes look on me, filled with concern. It isn't her or the baby. It's my mom calling me home. Instinctively, I know it's her. "Somethings happened," I say through gritted teeth. The pain becoming less, I straighten myself out. "Go, return to my world."

In the celebration, the liquid spirits, music, and dancing, I don't think anyone notices the portal I open taking myself home to Thraves. The place hasn't changed. The same pictures hang on the walls. My mom sits on the couch, her head drooped in her hands. My father isn't home but he wouldn't be. He works nights.

The relationship I have with my mom is strained to say the least. I hate her to my core, but fatherhood and the bond I share with my child softens me as I approach her. She lifts her head. Chestnut waves of hair fall over her shoulder and in that moment of sorrow I see a beautiful woman. One I've never noticed.

My gut clenches at the tears soaking her face. "What is it?"

"You came. My baby," she sobs, opening her arms for me to join her.

"What is it?"

Sniffling, she keeps her arms out, nearly begging me to join her. Reluctantly, I give her my hand, resting it in hers.

"Your father. He…he…passed to Tranquility."

I lift my hand from hers. Anger works its way through my soul, filling it with darkness. The edges are sharp as a scythe blade and jagged as its teeth. "What?! How?!"

"A harvesting accident," she says between choked sobs.

No, my dad is a desk jockey. He doesn't go out in the field. The chief. It is the chief. Darkness bubbles and swirls inside me, flaming and cold, burning like ice chunks clunking through my veins. I push the door wide open, slamming it hard against the hallway. It hangs from its top hinge as I storm the complex. Each of my footfalls a shake in the mountain. Glass breaks, things rattle as I march. Not a single harvester opens a door or peeps a head out.

Energy bursts and pops inside and around me, buzzing like electricity.

I release it into the veils. Cracks web across them like fractured glass. Mended fissures open and spread as my anger brews. Blackness swims in circles around me, extending inky appendages as guards rush me. Black shadows swallow them like the warlock at the academy.

I push the guards standing outside the chief's residence to the side with a sweep of my hand and force energy at them. It glues them to the corridor as shadows engulf them.

The chief's door swings open as I force a strong wind gust against it. If I hadn't been so angry at the moment I would have noticed his living room was the size of my parents' entire apartment. Energy crackles around me, crashing into the fine chandelier hanging from the ceiling. It swings back and forth, back and forth, crashing into the ceiling before it smashes to the floor, shards spreading and flying everywhere.

I seethe, my chest moves in and out in heavy, angry breaths. "Coward!" I shout.

My realm walker vision tells me he's huddled in a corner between his bed and nightstand. The door swings open as I force energy at it. The knob hits the wall with such force it sticks inside it. Creating a wind, I lift his thick form into the air. *Let us take him…* the shadows urge, their blackness circling him like prey. His legs dangle in the air. "You did it and you will pay!"

Words choke from his lips and stumble out as a garble. I don't know what he sees when he looks at me but I know he fears it. I see it in his face.

I want him to suffer and spend his life in the Otherworld. Squeezing harder, blackness surrounds my vision and his eyes pop in his head. A pain like that of a needle pierces my shoulder. I drop him and swing around. Energy radiates horizontally across the room.

A harvester stands at the door. The energy drives him backwards as he crashes into the hallway. The shadows hungrily swarm the guard, devouring him whole.

I reach over my shoulder and pull the short narrow tube from my shoulder. A dart. I thrust it into the chief's neck. "You can have him now," I say to the hungry shadows. They cover his body in darkness as they devour him.

I have crossed a line allowing, ordering, them to devour him. I am guilty. The swarming shadows belong to me. They are attached. Mine.

I open a portal and step into it, returning to my inbetween. It is going to get uglier, and Marilisa and the baby need to be safe. I have to get her out.

I find her pacing the meeting room when I return. Her eyes plead with me as the portal recedes. She rushes towards me, her eyes searching mine, and flings her arms around my neck. Peace calms my bitter heart.

I hold her tight, not wanting them to go. Not wanting the moment to end. What I feel is sticky, syrupy, happy and sad, pink and fuzzy. It's love, strong, vivid, and spirited. "It's time," I say, my arm around the back of her neck. The other holding her lower back. I kiss the top of her silky hair.

"You and Theios need to leave. Go to Lols and never return." This is the last time I'll see her. I won't be around to see my child grow up. I know that option. Have thought

about it. The possibility was always tucked in
the back of my mind like a nightmare.

30

The dart pushed enough poison into my veins that I pass out after Marilisa and Theios depart. I wake up to emptiness in my inbetween. I've become used to her footsteps, conversation, laughter, and companionship. I wake to her smile. Loneliness buries me in its depths. It radiates to my core.

I've never felt so alone and admit I am in love with my child and Marilisa. We are infinity, no beginning, no ending, forever circling.

I can't tell how much time has lapsed. My world never changes unless I change it.

Lamont... I head speak through the new comicay without a response. I hail him again. Nothing.

A sinister feeling crawls its eight legs into my gut and burrows. A sickly sensation sprouts and grows. Now I get it, why Lamont always got so upset when I didn't respond. I understand. My guts twists like a pretzel. I try my mom. No response. Inhaling deep, I steady the angry blood rushing through me. Lamont not answering is a possibility, but not my mom.

I take a seat, unable to stand as waves of nausea spin my world and cramps sting my belly. I double over in pain as wails and screams fill my ears. The veils crack like shells, lines spreading through every realm.

The steady thump of the realms beats like a sick, irregular heartbeat. The loneliness is hollow, void and deep, growing deeper. I realize it's not only Marilisa's absence. *Hackey, Shiane, Jine,* I call, hoping one will answer and the loneliness will fill, the steady thump will return, but it doesn't. It can't. They are all gone.

The worst thoughts race through my brain. She's dead, he's dead. They're all dead. My outrage killed them. The purebloods wanted complete control. They never planned to give us what they promised. *Hackey, Jine,* I call frantically. There's no response.

All the work we did, and the talk was to appease us, keep us calm, under their thumb.

No more! I portal to Lamont's family home. As the light vanishes, my eyes water at the sight. Wiping the tear forcing itself from my eye, I take Lamont's lifeless body in my arms and hold him to my chest. Like Ryel, he's gone. I can't even save his soul sphere. I imagine it bright violet like hers.

Regardless of our fight, Lamont was a true friend, my best friend.

A man I cared deeply for. He's gone, and so are his parents. His hand is curled tightly. I carefully pull back his fingers, revealing a metal pin in the shape of a triangle, a silver S embossed inside the triangle. I know that pin.

By the looks of the room, they fought. Chairs are knocked over, glass and tables broken. The place is a mess. I collect the family in an energy field, pushing my anger down while my mind plots a course of action. They won't get away with this. I bury their bodies in Lols, near Ryel.

Returning to Sier in dragon form, I go to the hybrids who designed the upgrade for the comicays. I find them as I did Lamont's family. Sorrow, not anger, pushes through me as I stare at Tamre's lifeless body. Her long, thick legs twisted in an unnatural fashion. This is too much.

Death. None deserved death, not for fighting for freedom and equality. The purebloods are no better than humans and their wasteful wars.

Beside Tamre on the floor is a blue cloth, another clue. I stuff it in my pocket with the pin. There is someone I can visit. A hybrid dragon who hasn't publicly embraced the movement, yet helped us, gave us intel. He won't be a target as he passes for pureblood.

Low lighting, music, and chatter overwhelm my senses as I walk into Mantel's club, deep in the belly of Sier. In dragon form I blend as I maneuver through the club, searching for Mantel. In a private booth tucked away from the masses of red and white-headed bulky dragons, I spot his fiery red braids and thick shoulders. I take the stone steps two at a time and face him.

Recognition doesn't hit him at first until I drop the glamour on my face for a second. A crooked smile crosses his as he invites me to sit with him.

"I know why you're here. I expected you'd come."

I pull the clues out of my pocket and unfurl my hand.

He doesn't study them long. "Yes, those belong to the covert supreme guard who are nothing more than glorified vigilantes. Not a group to be messed with."

His voice low, but in the corner tucked away from the crowd, the music is quiet and I hear every word.

"Where can I find them?"

He squares his shoulders as he leans into the back of the velvety loveseat. "Everywhere trouble is."

"They killed Lamont. Where can I find them?"

His eyes dart to the bar and rest on a white-haired dragon, the sides of his head shaved and the top and back tied into a pony tail. He looks rough, cocky, as he leans against the bar with a schmoozing woman on each side.

I stand and turn.

"The realm leaders have called for a cleansing of all realm walkers and they aren't stopping there," his words drift into my ear and I turn my head towards him and nod. I catch the drift. They are going after hybrids now and the older generation realm walkers if they aren't dead yet. None of us are safe, but I'll fix that. I have something dark and sharp shadowing me, something I don't want but accept. I alone have the power to right the wrongs and avenge deaths. To do that I'll have to give my tainted soul over to them completely.

31

I follow the self-assured covert guard, keeping a close eye on him as he stumbles with a dragon woman at his side. Using the listening skills Marilisa taught me, I tune into the chatter at the club and outside. Commoners fell through the fissures I created in my rage as I marched to the chief's home. The realm leaders and purebloods tremble and quake in terror. They blame us…me. They want me dead.

Inky black souls of wraiths swirl at the edges of my vision. I stalk the guard, waiting for the right moment. He pushes open a door and enters with the women. She is his flavor of the night and no harm will come to her.

I lean against the alley wall for several minutes before entering through the solid wall. I melt into it, my molecules moving through the crevices. I bubble wrap her in an energy field and portal her to the other side of Sier.

I enter the room. His shirt on the floor, an arm over her empty blouse on the bed. His eyes draw to me and fill with rage as I show myself. Is he angry I took his flavor of the night or at recognition as I am no longer in dragon form but my own? *We want him. Let us have him.* The voices chatter around me, slithering against my legs.

Not yet, I say, accepting my fate, accepting the wraiths as part of me.

She is only one. I need them all.

His eyes dart to the wall on my right. Not losing my focus, I move towards him. He pushes upward, wings spread outward on his back, stretching across the width of the room. Scales move over his body as a shield. Talons grow from his fingertips and a tail slashes a pillow from the bed. It drops to the floor.

I push energy at him, halting his shift. "Was it you?" I ask in a calm tone.

His chest heaves in and out and his talons scratch the invisible cage around him. His tail whips against the energy, causing ripples.

"I have time, but you don't." I force him against the wall. His wings crack against it, thundering in my ears. The shadows swarm around him as they come out to play, waiting for me to say yes.

His eyes bulge. The wraiths can't have him in my energy bubble, but I'll eventually give him to them. "Killing me won't stop the others," he says, the words dripping in hate.

"You're going to tell me where I can find the others."

His bulgy eyes narrow into seething slits. "No. I'll die first. You can torture me but I will not break my code of honor."

If I give him to the wraiths I'll gain another warrior, but I won't find the others. Then I remember the first wraith who entered me in the Otherworld. It read my thoughts. Can I use her? Do I have the strength to assist her in entering the dragon outside of the Otherworld?

I summon the original wraith. *Can you enter him like you did me?* Ripples move across the bubble as the dragon's tail thrashes and wings expand.

Only if I get to take his soul when I'm done. He's all yours.

Another line is crossed. I made a deal with a wraith, one I allowed in me, to inhabit me. Bargains with wraiths don't have happy endings.

Realm Walker

From the mass of circling blackness a singular form pushes from the center. I drop my energy shield and the dragon completes his shift. He flies toward the ceiling carved from the mountain and turns, head low, wings back. Like a bullet he drives towards me.

Red glows from the murky shadow. The dragon doesn't slow. I don't think it sees the wraith. Blackness twists around his body. The dragon opens his mouth to shoot ice at me. The wraith takes that as an invitation to slither inside him. Her dark form vanishes and the dragon chokes and coughs. I jump out of the way as it drops to the floor. Its heft shakes the walls.

The dragon seizes and writhes. Its tail thrashes, then it stops. Its shoulders and back straighten and crack as the wraith takes control, its eyes glowing red. A twisted smile erupts on the dragon's face as he marches past me.

The gathering shadows follow us. I am building an army of wraiths. On some unconscious level, I've known it. They are attached to me but my power only extends to them as long as I don't give them a body. Instantly realizing my mistake, I have no choice but to hope the wraith does as I asked.

Loyal to me and hungry for more souls, she leads me and the wraith army to every covert supreme guard. Their souls devoured by the mob of wraiths. With each soul, the army grows and their strength builds in me. I am stronger, invincible. More lines crossed.

The last of the guard is swallowed by the insatiable army. I face the wraith. "It's time."

"What's in it for me?" it asks.

The shadows teem between us, feeding off the negative energy. Without her inside me she can't read my mind… So I lie. I have to give her something, a promise, so she will do as I ask. Inside a physical form she has less power, but can be more dangerous and continue building the wraith army until there's no one left. Inside me, I can control its appetite, but I have to give up myself. Anything in me worth saving will be destroyed, but I can't force her out of the dragon. I need to give her something she wants.

"After we go to every realm and wipe out those responsible for the deaths of the realm walkers, I'll let you choose a permanent host."

Anyone?

I nod. If she chooses me, I'm dead anyways. My soul more than tainted. It's black and murky.

Black splotches mottle the skin of the dragon guard as she consumes him from the inside out. I have no plans for her to assume a form and continue building the army.

It has to stop once all those who are guilty are destroyed. A bridge I'll cross when the time is right.

As each of the guilty souls are overcome, the resulting wraiths give themselves a name and my power doubles, triples.

They call themselves the *Council of Divination* and I remember the man's words in my vision in the Abandoned Desert in Drakonia. He claimed this and I'm living it. I admire the name, as it is exactly what they are. A council I created to "cleanse" the wrong doers of the evil they brought on the realms.

32

I send out the wraiths to find my mother's killer. I saved Thraves for last. A place I once called home. The army returns to me like a flock of birds and the first wraith obediently devours the fae whose body she assumed in Navarin. I won't give her another body to consume and will pay the wraith whatever the price.

Inside the heart of Crest, below CIU, I seek the harvester who killed my mother. As realm walkers, we are powerful but not immortal. I felt her pain and her peace as she entered Tranquility.

Let me take her to find the others…

Realm Walker

Not yet.

What are you waiting for?

The council swarms outside my body, their shadows a trail of darkness covering the floor. I don't respond to the wraith. Staying guarded, I create an energy bubble around me to protect myself from death.

It won't be my time until I avenge every realm walker death, including the mother I never got along with.

It's strange, in her death I remembered good times. How she beamed the first time I created wind. It made her proud. How she fixed my favorite snack after harvesting school. The first time she took me to Mer Point to watch the mermaids.

I ignored our connection but I think she always felt it, like I feel a thin cord to my child.

Crest is a clever place for my mother's assassin to hide out. There are many tunnels and caves. But I am a realm walker. I see beyond walls and borders.

I don't need the wraith to find the elite here. I know Thraves as the realm walker of the realm.

I pick off a stalactite and fashion a sharp sword. It glows in my hand. Its energy diffusing through my arm. The energy in the corridor changes, softens. It envelopes me in a familiar warmth.

You don't need that.

You had all the others. This one is mine. I will hold true to my promise, I say to the wraith.

"Cyrus," says the sweetest, purest voice. I turn on my heel. Marilisa stands a few feet from me. Our connection has diminished since the baby was born, but no doubt that is how she found me. I told her to go. To not return no matter what. The baby is more important than either of us. The veils won't hold without a realm walker. Merla's spell warned they will fall if any realm walker is harmed.

Her long hair trimmed below her shoulders, her eyes shining from the light of my stalactite sword. I urge, "You can't be here!"

"I am. I've felt everything you've gone through. Sensed the pain of each realm walker as they perished. I can't…" Tears simmer in the corners of her eyes. "I have to fight alongside you. Terra is safe with Theios." She smiles. "She's beautiful and we found the perfect home for her. A place she will always fit in."

My thoughts of the wraiths and everything else vanishes. "A girl. We have a girl?"

She nods. "A perfect girl."

I drop my energy shield and run to her. I want to fill my arms with her, hold on and not let go. She is the woman who birthed the future savior of the middle realms, of life.

The child whose strong, pure soul will return Ryel to me. The last part of the thought seems foreign. My energy focused on Ryel for so many months but when the baby became a reality, when Marilisa and I… Serenity grew in the months of peace and Marilisa's pregnancy but now…strife fills the lands.

"You have to stop this," she begs.

"I can't. They all must perish for what they've done."

Her skin soft as she collects my hands. "No. If this continues everything will fall apart and even our child won't be able to save it." Her head drops forward, landing on my shoulder. I fold my arms around her, feel her body against mine. It feels right. I press my lips against her head when a stinging sensation, hot, red, and sticky brushes my arm. I lift my head and see an arrow impaled in her back, mirroring her heart. Blood drains from the wound. She chokes, her body shakes. *Not again! No!*

Both my loves met the same fate. My love is toxic, poison.

I visually trace the arrow's trajectory and see a matching arrow moving towards my face. It's centered between my eyes. *Let me enter and we will take the vigilante as we have the others,* the wraith begs.

"No!" My voice reverberates off the cave walls and sorrow fills my heart. In that moment the arrow freezes mid-air. Time halts.

I force my energy toward Marilisa to contain her soul.

The wraith army heads toward the vigilante as the original wraith pleads: *Let me have her. You are reneging on your promise!*

The council devours the harvester. I can't give it her soul. She would live, but wouldn't be her.

I gave up my soul, but it was never as pure and sweet as hers. I decide what to do. The only thing I can to save her soul and send the wraith back to the Otherworld.

I let go of the energy I'm using to contain her soul. Time moves again and I step to the side. The arrow whizzes past me, hitting the cave wall and knocking a stalactite off the ceiling. It shatters on impact.

I hold her in my arms. Her eyes roll and breath rattles. "Do it," she says, as if she can hear my conversation with the wraiths. She probably can. I wonder if she knows what I'm going to do. Her hand touches my unshaven, stubbled face. "I love…you."

Blood pours over my arm. It's wet and warm. I fight the tears welling in my eyes. I nod for the wraith to enter. Once she's inside, I use energy to shove my stalactite blade into Marilisa's heart.

You betrayed me! The wraith shouts obscenities. Harvester 101: an inhabiting wraith's weakness is death of the inhabited body. Once it dies, their form returns to the Otherworld.

A tar-like sphere rises from Marilisa's body, its form shapes and reshapes as it fights within itself in an attempt to halt its descent to the Otherworld. A bright light emerges. The tar cracks like an egg and blue light shines.

The cave walls illuminate with its brilliance. The black tar falls away and reforms as it descends. I wipe at my tears and joy floods me. I watch as Marilisa ascends to Tranquility.

The cave grows dark, shadows swarm and circle her sphere. The army descends on her like serpents. No! They can't have her!

I swallow hard. A lump forms in my stomach and the joy vanishes. It's too late for Ryel. Her soul will never go to Tranquility. She, too, may be tainted like me, because of me and my desperation to save her. My first love, I couldn't let her go, didn't love her enough. I remember her full laugh, see her running through the snow as a white wolf and the moonlight bright on her blonde, springy curls.

I am as vile as the wraiths that inhabit me, worse than them. I let them in, all of them. I crossed all the lines. My deaths, my blood, my pain and penance, but not the women I love.

Memories of Marilisa flood me. Our arguments, our dissension, her scent, teaching me how to listen to the trees, telling me my ideas reek worse than toadflax. Her soft skin against my hands, listening and touching her rounded belly, her laughter, and the peachy, cotton candy warmth she brought my tortured, tainted soul.

Stinking of black death and hateful shadows of unharvested unrested souls, I am the death of my loves. Just as I couldn't give Ryel a second chance as a vampire, a form that would have killed her soul, I can't let them have Marilisa, changing her into something shadowy and evil. Her soul is pure. My guiding light. "You can't have her!"

I wrap energy around her soul and tug. They tug, she wobbles, moving more their direction than mine. I pull harder, drawing all the available energy. I can't let Ryel's fate be hers. Marilisa's sphere moves towards me, slowly.

Shadow fingers reach and I pull. She's closer, almost close enough. A little more. I almost have her. I take a step backwards. My foot catches on the rim of the rocky bridge I'm standing on. I flounder only for a second, but it's enough they pull her towards them.

"No!" I scream as I push a blast of energy at them. They scatter and she drops. Blue light shines against the cave as she falls. I drop and slide forward before she can get through the gap between the wall and bridge. My hands reaching, one between the gap to catch her. I swing the other over to cover her.

When her sphere touches my hand it zaps, sending cold energy circulating into me, and throws me backwards. I slide several feet as her sphere falls between the crack and keeps falling. Her light shines against the walls and I watch through the crack.

Wraiths descend. I can't let them have her. I have already given my soul to them. I didn't think of it a moment ago, but now I do. They are my wraiths attached to my soul. My soul, their tar-pit.

I call them home. Blackness fills me and their hate prickles with heat as they coil inside me. I am them and they are me. I choke as their goo slides down my throat blocking my airwaves. They writhe like worms baking in the sun.

I am them and they are me. The dark souls of all those I killed and had killed. They are my eternal punishment.

The arrow meant for me lies on the rocky bridge, teetering into the oblivion below. I rub my fingers, creating a flame, and burn it into ash.

My tirade of vengeance created an army that will wait with me until I figure out how to destroy it. They call me the Vile One. They hate me for sending the first back to the Otherworld.

The stalactite blade drops as my foot pushes against it. I pick it up and hold it to my chest and push, it breaks the skin. Drops of blood trail downward over my flesh. If I kill myself with all the wraiths inside me they will all be sent to the Otherworld and I will suffer a miserable existence. It's what I deserve.

I press harder, the sting feels good… right. My hand flies away, losing its grip on the stalactite. It crashes against the cave wall and thuds and tinks as it drops into the crevice with Marilisa's blue lost soul sphere.

They won't let me.

I don't see the glow from her sphere for me to collect it and put it on the shelf next to Ryel's. She can be reverse harvested and sent to Tranquility if it's not too late. I can't. My soul is dirty.

She fought for Tranquility. I fought with her. In the struggle, we both lost.

REALM WALKER

33

The cleansing erased from memories, the council of divination whispers to any who listen. They murmur and conspire in my ears and soul. The purebloods finish Provence and form a tribunal, as if that will erase their guilt. Over the many years, Provence sees changes. The Hall finishes, Provence square is built, much smaller than we imagined, the mall, and houses are erected.

Each realm elects, or chooses according to their laws, five purebloods to represent their realm on the tribunal as a diplomat. They are provided one of the homes in Provence to live in during their service.

I think it was need more than want that brought the changes. Without realm walkers to do the work and go between realms, they had to compromise.

Hybrids aren't granted any rights but they are allowed to live in peace within the realms so long as they don't cause trouble. The hybrids showed themselves to be formidable. That memory and fear bent the realm leaders enough they leave them alone.

The City is built with representation of each realm, and eventually the school is erected in the location below the curtain I created to Lols. The curtain hides on the fourth floor.

Realm walkers are wiped from history, books containing any knowledge of them taken off shelves and destroyed. The cleansing never spoken of.

My daughter is growing up in a land with little magic. She herself knows nothing of any of it. A normal commoner girl, a powerful secret hiding within.

A part of me yearns to collect her, teach her how to be a realm walker, but I won't endanger her life. She is happy with Theios. He is a good father to her. I don't visit because it isn't only the purebloods that concern me but the council of divination lockstep with my soul.

Realm Walker

I hide as a troll. It is the easiest form for me to keep for extended periods of time. I make a name for myself in Verboten. My true self – Cyrus – is a legend in any circle that dares speak my name.

Provence isn't exactly what we wanted, but peace exists. Serenity never recovered from what I or the realm leaders did, but her diminishing did slow.

The veils bear the cracks of war. They try to repair them, but those fixes are temporary.

I hope for enough time. Time for Terra's power to grow until it matches or overcomes mine. My soul dead, she is the only true living realm walker and her soul will one day be put to the test with a string of challenges only she can unravel.

My precious, pure soul who will save the souls and lives of many. She is the gold who will continue what I started. Maybe she can even vanquish the council of divination.

I scoff as my little troll feet walk past the fountain of Provence Academy. A back-to-back lycan and dragon fountain. The heavy doors brandishing pickaxe handles. Dean Salena, with her bobbed fuchsia hair tucked behind her pointed fae ears, welcomes me to the academy as an instructor of magic.

To be continued…

Soul of Malice

Suggested Realm Walker reading order:

These reading orders are suggestions only. Try one out or find your own.

Enjoy the Ah Ha moments (order written by author)
In the Shadows
The Land of Lost Souls
The Origin: Marya's Journal
Hidden Passages
Soul Fire
The Ring of Betrayal
Heart of Darkness
Soul of Malice
Life after Death

To thoroughly enjoy the HFN
In the Shadows
The Land of Lost Souls
The Origin: Marya's Journal
Hidden Passages
Soul Fire
Heart of Darkness
Soul of Malice
Life after Death
Ring of Betrayal

The prequels can also be read first and Life After Death last.

LIFE AFTER DEATH

Sneak peak!

ottles clank against each other in the cloth bag Sulien carries. A griffin snorts in the distance. Its sound distinct and ethereal. In the middle mountains the air is always chilly in the morning. All that defines day and night in Marsidia is the temperature and moisture.

Above the fog line is cold and wet. The warlocks living high in the mountains use the clouds and moisture to their advantage. It is hardy living. Those who live below the fog line, like Sulien, aren't as small-community oriented and more political.

He places a large boot on the first wooden step. At nearly seven feet tall, he isn't a small man. The second step groans under his weight. Not particularly heavy for his height. The last step protests as he raises his hand to knock.

The door swings open before his fist hits the wood. "You're just in time. I used my last on tea this morning."

Sulien lowers the cloth bag to the table and drops the handles. They fall against the sides of the bag, revealing two large jars of sap. Sap is a great business for Sulien. The trees on his land overflow with it. Some have medicinal value, while others prevent the wear and tear of warlock aging, yet others assist with temperament. The flavors and uses aren't any more the trees than magic gifts granted to him by the source.

It is the sentient center of magic. All magic. He is a healer of sorts, but not always through conventional methods. Some gifts are better not spoken of. His customers don't know of his forbidden magic. Yet his magic, like all magic, is bequeathed to him through the source. It is the things not spoken of that others fear. Therefore, he keeps his abilities to himself and customers keep their orders coming on a regular basis.

Magic has a balance to it. It isn't merely the runes the source provides. The marks linked to their abilities, carefully crafted skills imbued to each warlock.

Felan is a small woman. Her long, golden hair braided with a ribbon that runs the length of her spine, and eyes the color of amber. She is a beautiful woman. She invites him to sit down and enjoy a tea before his journey home. It isn't but a good thirty-minute journey on foot. He doesn't mind, and often stays a few minutes when his customers request it.

Seran, her seven-year-old daughter, tugs at her mom's arm, her golden curls bouncing with sad excitement. "Mommy." Her eyes bubbling in wetness.

Felan's eyes turn toward the child. "What is it?"

"The shrike I found. It's not moving. It's dead." Her tiny voice worried and torn with sadness.

Sulien stands and walks to the cage. The tiny animal sits on the bottom in the leaf clutter, its feet tucked under its blue and green feathered body, eyes closed. "No dear, I'm sure it's only napping," he says and pushes a hand under his hair, pulling out a strand. Quietly, under his breath so the child and her mother can't hear, he utters to the small, feathery, beaked animal, "Death isn't the end of your life. It is the beginning."

The animal fluffs its feathers as if waking from a slumber.

"It was napping!" the girl exclaims, joy pushing away the sadness.

Sulien smiles at the girl then turns to Felan. "It's time I leave. Thank you for the tea. Until next week."

She smiles, unsure exactly what he did or if he did anything, and bids him a good afternoon.

The midday air warms his skin. The source has given him the ability to bring life back from death in animals. It isn't a skill he shares with others. The villagers have their suspicions. So long as he provides them sap to fill their needs, they don't talk.

It takes sacrifice for such strong magic to occur. It is *the* forbidden skill. Necromancy is feared in all of Marsidia. In the case of the shrike, he'd used a plug of his hair. The sacrifice depends on the ask.

"The patient is almost recovered," Leif states as Sulien enters the lab beneath his home. The stone walls keep it cool, tools of his trade litter the long stone table where he cultivates the sap with spells and alchemy. Recently, he'd found a griffon with an injured foot and brought him home to the lab. A few days of healing sap and it is nearly ready to leave. It purrs as Sulien pets its soft head and rubs behind its ears.

Leif runs a hand through his short, dirty-blond hair. "I don't think he wants to leave." The griffon brushes his head against Leif's hands, urging him to pet him.

"We've made a lifelong friend," Sulien utters as he smooths the velvety fur of the griffon. Its plumose tail sweeps the worn stone floor, pushing dirt with it.

REALM WALKER

In the evening, the colorful lights
pulse through the air and an evening chill
swells through the open windows. Leif sets
two plates at the table. He's been his assistant
since he was orphaned. Sulien hadn't made it
to his parents in time and they died. Leif was
ten and had nowhere to go and Sulien needed
an assistant. He'd trained him over the years
and their relationship grew. Not only is it a
working relationship, and a good one but
Sulien, is a surrogate dad.

Sulien's brows furrow and he meets
Leif's gaze as a knock on the door interrupts
their meal of steaming broth loaded with
vegetables and chunks of meat. The rich
aroma of earthy spices filling their nostrils.
Sulien closes his eyes and shakes his head as
Leif pushes out his chair. The hefty wooden
door opens with a creak.

Two sentries in navy uniforms with
gold-trimmed edges on the collar stand on the
porch. Their posture straight and unwavering
like ancient tree trunks. Stern looks painted
on their faces. They lack any emotion or
decency for interrupting the meal. Do they go
home to their families with the grim faces
they always wear?

As warrior warlocks they are chosen
because of their speed, agility runes, strength,
and cunning. Ones that make them good
fighters. Once a year, during the trials, they
choose new sentries. All Marsidia watches

them fight one another with magic. It's frightening and mesmerizing as equally matched warriors duck and punch. Streams of magic billow from their hands, fashioned into weapons of destruction. The most skilled, or those who survive, are chosen.

A rising thrum of voices mingled with marching feet rings in his ears. Sulien's heart sinks as he joins Leif at the door, studying the sentries and growing throng of townspeople. So many familiar faces sullen and angry. His heart breaks in two. These people are his clients. He's delivered them sap for all things over the years and now they look on him with horror in their eyes.

The shorter sentry, a female, meets his gaze. Her dark eyes studying his, her dark hair cropped above her ears. Runes peek out from the cloth on her neck. "Which of you is Sulien the sap maker?" Her unyielding tone matches her steely gaze.